Exploits of an Underpaid Supernatural Bartender

Exploits of the Hellhound-verse

Charles M. Brown

Published by Hellhound's Run Books, 2024.

This is a work of fiction. Similarities to real people, places, or events are entirely coincidental.

EXPLOITS OF AN UNDERPAID SUPERNATURAL BARTENDER

First edition. November 4, 2024.

Copyright © 2024 Charles M. Brown.

ISBN: 979-8227666918

Written by Charles M. Brown.

Table of Contents

I Met Cthulu's Illegitimate Love Child 1
I Met The Man Who Hunts Cthulu's Illegitimate Love Child 12
I Met a Sleep Paralysis Demon 23
Tim the Cursed 32
Necro Business 38
Gurk 47
Barista Vision 50
Curious Things 59
The Owner, The Priestess, and The Fool 66
Aftermath 77
I Met a Vampire 81
I Met A Blob's Chauffeur 86
Curious Introductions 91
Curious Statuary 106
Definitely Not Haunted 114
Slithering Matchmaker: | First Day 131
Find More Books In The Hellhound-verse | Visit Hellhoundsrun.com 138

Laughter is the best love in the universe.

I Met Cthulu's Illegitimate Love Child

My name is Dave, and I have a story I need to share. I work at the Hellhound Bar. I'm there every day and now that I think about it, I can't remember ever working anywhere else. We get some strange people who wander through here. After all, with a name like the Hellhound Bar, it's not a place that draws the trendier crowds. Honestly, I'm not sure ordinary everyday people can even find the place.

The bar has that quaint half-cloaked in shadow atmosphere that you usually find in places where it's better to mind your business. With a few old wooden tables, a long wooden bar, and an ancient jukebox; it was a place made for hard drinking and darker things. The bar has what seems to be the requisite long mirror half obscured by bottles of alcohol of every age, type, and variety. Stuff no one ever mentioned in bartending school to be sure.

Every day I come in, open the bar, and every surface is spotless and shining in the deep gloom. Come to think of it, I've never seen who cleans the bar or stocks it. It's always the same, every day I open. I asked the owner one time about the cleaning staff and he curtly told me to mind my own business or lose my soul. A bit extreme but I've had worse bosses.

It was a rainy Tuesday and I was working behind the polished oak bar when I saw a man walk through the wooden door causing the small bell above it to jingle lightly. The customer was covered head to foot in an old worn brown trench coat and a wide brimmed brown hat pulled low over his face. My first thought was, oh boy another weirdo. I had no idea how right and so very wrong I was in that one thought.

As the customer sat on one of the stools at the bar, I walked over to him and asked, "what'll it be"?

"Bourbon straight", the stranger said in a weird and exceedingly deep burbling voice. He didn't look up.

Now firmly believing this was going to be another one to watch I said, "you got it", and poured two fingers of middle shelf bourbon into a glass tumbler. The customer tipped it back quickly so that I couldn't make out his face under the hat before setting the glass on the bar and asking for another. There weren't many customers in the bar so after the fourth time he slammed the bourbon like a cheap shot of tequila, I tried to gently intervene.

"Whoa dude, slow down a little the bottle isn't going anywhere", I said with a small laugh. The mysterious customer looked up at me, his eyes just visible under the brim of his hat.

"Dave, I'll drink as fast as I damn well want to." His tone wasn't angry really but his voice resonated with a command I didn't understand and yet felt on a gonadal level. Stunned from this, I looked at the rather ominous dun-covered dude and saw his eyes for the first time. I mean, really saw his eyes. They glowed red! Now, I don't know a lot, but eyes shouldn't be glowing or red! That might be a clue that there was a problem here.

Instead of getting the hint, all I could think to ask was, how did he know my name? He continued to glare at me until

I thought I might just have to run screaming out of the bar before beginning to laugh in this deep voice. His voice was filled with sibilant hissing and burbling like the biggest loogie known to man was stuck in his throat.

"I'm just messing with you man", he said while continuing his hissing burbling laugh. It was like the guy was laughing, talking, and hissing all at the same time.

"My human name is Daniel. I just wanted to have a little fun", he said, "my life is so devoid of normal things I just wanted to see your reaction." Thinking a film crew was going to jump out any minute and say it was a prank I decided I would play along.

"Your human name, huh", I mumbled. "What is your nonhuman name", I asked stupidly.

He looked at me very pointedly before saying, "Dany'lehth". At the uttering of this one garbled word the floor of the bar shook and the gloom seemed to thicken. In the back, drunk old Mickey fell off of his stool. Pissing in the floor again, I was sure. Great. Why did I choose a career where people pissed themselves? Thinking about just how weird this truly was, I instantly went into smart alec mode.

"Gesundheit", I said before I could stop myself. Daniel's shoulders shook with mirth as he hissed out the words, "good one", and continued that strange laugh/hiss thing. It was seriously creepy.

"So, what's your story dude", I asked. Honestly, I wasn't sure what Pandoras Box of nightmares I was opening up with this question, but hey, I was bored. Daniel looked at me for a moment before replying.

"I am Cthulu's illegitimate love child", he said in disgust before slamming back another bourbon. Now, I'd expected a lot of answers. Cheating wife, lost job, just about any response except that. Who says something like that anyway? I stood there dumbly, holding a rag in one hand and an empty glass in the other. My simple mind just could not process this statement. I felt like all my gerbils had just gone on strike.

"Huh", I muttered, thus winning the great conversationalist award of all time.

"I am Cthulu's illegitimate love child", he repeated, "and I really really hate my dad". At this point I knew I had to be on a game show or had hit my head and was enjoying a nice stay in the coma ward at Saint Luc's. Before I could respond, Daniel continued, "do you have any idea of the issues you have when your dad is a tentacle monster from the outer realms?"

Being the natural smart ass I am, all I could say was, "guess your mom liked hentai huh?"

Daniel stared at me under the brim of his hat, his eyes glowing brighter and brighter until I felt like his stare would melt me into the floor before he began bellowing in laughter and slammed back his sixth bourbon like a frat girl at spring break. He continued to laugh, and hiss as I slowly exhaled and thanked every deity I could think of, he thought the comment was funny.

"Hentai, huh", he asked, "maybe that's what she meant when she said Dad had touched her like no other being."

"Oh, gross dude", I exclaimed but couldn't help chuckling at the sheer sickness of the comment. I'd started it so I might as well ride it out.

"No man, seriously, my dad is such a dick", Daniel proclaimed. "Like when I was sixteen, I fell in love with this girl and he said she wasn't good enough because she wasn't insane, didn't hear voices, and had never sacrificed anyone to the Elder Gods. I mean really, is that any way to judge who I can date?"

Shaking my head and feeling really confused all I could utter was another epically loquacious "huh" in response. Eloquence, thy name is Dave the Bartender. After standing stunned for a moment the gerbils seemed to lock onto something insignificant to continue the conversation with. Bloody stupid gerbils!

"Ok", I said, "you're talking about the Cthulu from the books right?"

"You're new here, huh", Daniel asked, looking me over pityingly. He picked up his seventh bourbon, and I noticed that the skin on his hand was grey. Not a normal color but the grey of a corpse that had been in the water for way too long. I swallowed loudly after seeing this and wondered if there was any possible chance Daniel was telling the truth. Or had I finally made it to a psych ward and when would the jello arrive? Daniel did not seem like he wanted to pursue the subject further so I decided to enjoy the hallucination.

"If your dad is Cthulu how can you be illegitimate," I asked. Daniel chuckled softly.

"My dad doesn't really do labels and adores the idea of chaos, so marriage isn't his style." Daniel shook his head and continued, "besides, there aren't as many universes as there used to be and dad really couldn't afford to devour another one just to establish an outer realm marriage ceremony." This conversation just keeps getting weirder I thought to myself.

6

"Devour another universe", I asked a little shakily.

"Yeah", Daniel said, "apparently it's a custom of the chaos realms that at least one universe must be devoured and all life destroyed as part of the wedding feast." I could hear Daniel's heavy phlegmy sigh as he rolled his eyes. He accidentally tilted his head upward towards the light when he rolled his eyes. I couldn't not stare. Honestly, I tried! What I had originally thought was a thick mustache looked like thin tubes that were...they were......moving!

"Are those tentacles", I blurted disbelievingly.

"No Dave, it's a porn 'stache", he replied defensively, "yes they're tentacles, you idiot! My dad's friggin' Cthulu you ass!" As his voice rose the bar began to shake again and bottles fell off the shelves behind me. Feeling my butthole pucker so hard I thought I'd be turned inside out I quickly apologized.

"I'm sorry, I'm sorry", I blurted in a panicky rush. And just like that the shaking stopped and the air returned to normal. Feeling like I could breathe again and promising myself I would murder the person who had slipped 'shrooms in my coffee when I came down, I poured Daniel yet another bourbon. Did he even feel the alcohol?

"No, I'm sorry Dave", he said somewhat contritely. "I'm just a little touchy about my appearance. All my life I've just wanted to be normal", he continued dejectedly, "but noooo, not me. My dad has to be the tentacled god of madness and despair."

For a moment I thought he might weep, but then he shook himself and slammed back another bourbon. Seriously, the dude had to have three livers! The whole bar was silent as I kind of did a half push up off the bar. The scene was just so surreal. Out of nowhere Mickey, the old drunk, stumbled up behind

Daniel. The smell hit us both at the same time and I almost wretched. The smell of sour piss and old bourbon made my eyes water.

"Lawd, my lawd", Mickey slurred as he fell to his knees beside Daniel. "Lawd let me worsshhhiiipppp", Mickey whimpered from below the bar.

"Not again", Daniel said, gagging from the smell and sighed loudly. His sigh seemed to come from the darkness of the gloomy bar and infect the soul. I did not want to throw Mickey out. Don't get me wrong, he was a horrible old drunk and no one liked having him there, but I really didn't want to touch him. The last time I had escorted him out I felt like I needed a body condom. But, he was bothering a paying customer so...

I started to move around the bar, determined to lose my sense of smell when Daniel raised his hand in a motion for me to stop. And I did. I didn't want to stop, I just suddenly couldn't move forward.

"Leave him" Daniel said. In that moment he looked so tired, or at least, his glowing red eyes did.

"Wha-", I started to ask and froze again. A loud boom echoed from the rear of the bar and I could hear screams and sirens in the distance. It suddenly sounded like there was a riot in the distance. Before I could think about the sounds from outside a blonde tornado of junkie in leopard print screamed into the bar towards Daniel and Mickey. As the dervish of disgusting slid to a stop beside Mickey I recognized Wanda. Wanda was a back alley lady, to put it as nicely as possible.

"Great", I blurted, "is this a meeting of the deranged or what"? Wanda was whimpering and clinging to Daniel's leg. It looked like she was grinding against him like a stripper with Tourette's.

"Dude, what is going on", I yelled.

"This happens", Daniel said, looking back at me from the sobbing prostitute and before trailing off.

"What happens", I asked, "you attract crazy people like puppies"?

"Well, yeah, kind of", he said before looking back down at the writhing forms.

"Well, just don't ask if you can keep them. I mean, did your mom ever have to tell you, 'no you can't keep the crazy people and no they didn't just follow you home' when you were a child?" Daniel snorted softly and the walls seemed to waver a little. 'Shrooms, man, had to be 'shrooms.

"Take me, I'll bear the children of lunacy on this very bar for you", Wanda muttered to Daniel from her position on the floor.

Suddenly, a wet splatter hit my cheek and a soft thump filled the bar. I stood stunned, shaken by what I had just seen. Mickey had lurched up from the floor, grabbed an empty beer bottle and used it like a cop's truncheon on Wanda's skull. Wanda lay there, her legs twitching as Mickey screamed words at Daniel. It took a minute for the gerbils to kick in the drunk guy translator portion of my brain.

"I will have your babies", Mickey screamed at Daniel. He sank back to his knees, the bottle sliding from his hands. "I will have your baby s, oh Lord of Chaos", Mickey slurred before falling over in Wanda's blood. I didn't know what was worse, the look of Daniel frozen in horror at the old man's proclamation, Wanda's body spasming on the floor of the bar, or Mickey lying in Wanda's blood puking into his beard.

"What the- what the- what is happening". I screamed.

"Look, Dave, it's all my dad's fault. I just don't like talking about it", Daniel said and looked at me with his eyes glowing red.

"Well, I think it's time to talk about it", I said. Daniel froze in front of me and time stopped. I don't mean it felt like time stopped. Time literally stopped, even the ticking of the clock above the bar stopped. After maybe 20 non-seconds of facing Daniel's stare and realizing that my life had been pretty pathetic up to this point, and that I didn't want to die here, Daniel agreed.

"Ok", he said and kind of straddled the barstool above the two inert forms while signaling for another bourbon. What was this, his tenth or maybe twelfth?

"My dad isn't from this reality", Daniel said, "and something about his children cause things to happen everywhere we go". Daniel shifted slightly, "everywhere I go followers, batshit crazy people to be honest, spring up and start trying to sacrifice the world in my honor. People I talk to go mad and cut their faces off. Some peoples' whole lives change for the worse when I'm around". Daniel snorted before continuing, "one normal guy named Hunter and I were talking in the park. The next week he's died, come back, and is bound by some curse to hunt me and people like me. A lady I asked out one time, she was a writer, suddenly has a seizure, goes into a coma, and now any story she tells comes true like some ancient oracle". He heaved a huge sigh and downed his bourbon.

"Something about being half human and half Younger God makes everything just go wrong", he said with an introspective air.

"No, really"?I said, lookeing down at his feet. Daniel looked to the ground and looked back up at me. He opened his eyes to say something and the world exploded. Not literally, I mean come on you're reading this. But the world inside the bar seemed to come apart. The door flew open so hard it shot the little bell above it to the rear of the bar like a shotgun blast. The few dirty windows near the door just evaporated into dust.

I couldn't hear anything but I could feel a thrumming sound so deep in my chest I thought my ribs would come loose from my sternum. My last clear memory is of Daniel flinging off his coat and hat. His skin was corpse grey and seemed to writhe along his body. His tentacle porn 'stache flared as he charged out the door screaming, "damnit dad, not again".

I don't know how long I was unconscious on the floor of the bar. I woke up lying face down with my cheek glued to the wooden floor from years of spilled liquids and who knows what else. I could feel something sharp poking me in my ribs and rolled over to see the bar's owner poking me with a broom handle. I grunted at him and waved my arms to fend off the stick. I probably looked as graceful as a retarded baby T-rex doing it.

"Well, you're not dead", the owner snarled at me. "Guess I would have lost that bet", he said to the empty bar. I slowly got to my feet and took stock. All my parts were there. Looking around I saw that the door and windows had been repaired.

"How long have I been out", I asked, turning towards the owner.

"About five minutes. Now get back to work", he said and snorted.

"Five minutes", I stated, "that's not possible. Everything is fixed, the bodies are gone, there's no way, what happened?" I was close to panic. The owner had turned to walk away but stopped and looked back over his shoulder at me.

"Family squabbles happen among the Younger Ones, now get back to work". I stopped, and I mean I stopped dead. The owners eyes, they glowed. Just like Danie ls. They glowed!

I Met The Man Who Hunts Cthulu's Illegitimate Love Child

My name is Dave and you might remember me as the bartender at the Hellhound Bar. I thought the last story would be the only one I'd have to tell but here I am again. Honestly, I'm not sure what would happen if the owner ever found out I was sharing these stories, but I don't think he'd be too pleased. After what I saw the last time I'm concerned but, really, who would believe me anyway? Anyone reading this would think I was just a bad writer who couldn't find original material.

Weird things just keep happening. Working here is strange enough. I mean, every afternoon when I open I feel like I'm being watched. I keep hearing these weird gurgling sounds from under the bar Last night I was closing the bar when I saw a puddle of beer spilled on the floor. Normally I'd wipe it up but I was out on my feet. Some of the patrons had decided to light their darts on fire to make the annual dart tournament more competitive. Normally I would have mopped up the spill, but I thought I could just do it in the morning. It's not like the floor doesn't have a lot of stains already, though I've never figured out why most of them are dark brown, I mean, we don't sell wine… Anyway, this morning, I came in to find one of my clean bar rags pinned to the bar with a rusty knife. The rag was covered in what smelled like old beer. Weird, right?

Anyway, it's been about a week since the whole thing with Daniel, and I was finally managing to convince myself it had never happened. I mean, tentacle hentai monsters just don't exist, right? It was another slow Tuesday afternoon. Mickey was sitting in the booth stinking up the corner by the front door and I was half wiping the bar and daydreaming about the girl at the church down the street. I'm not one for religion but even I had a problem with the concept of the Church of the Goldfish.

Standing behind the bar in a semi-daze; I wasn't focused on the door. Which is when it flew open, making a screeching sound before slamming into the wall. I jumped and maybe screamed a little. Thankfully the slam of the door against the wall drowned it out. Silhouetted in the doorway was a tall figure. His long coat blew in the breeze from outside as he waited in the doorway like some dime store novel hero. I don't know what possessed Mickey, but he jumped up yelling like all of hell was on his heels and charged at the silhouetted figure.

I honestly thought Mickey was going to run right through the guy and knock him down. Instead, the figure punched Mickey dead in his face. Remember those old cartoons where the character gets punched and the head stops but the feet keep going? Yeah, it was like that. The meaty thud of old whino crashing onto the polished wood made me wince as Mickey hit the ground. The figure in the doorway didn't flinch, no reaction at all.

After a few seconds the figure stepped over Mickey into the bar. He used his foot to shove Mickey's body out of the way and closed the door. As my eyes adjusted from the glaring portal of light back to the normal gloom, I could see the figure was a tall thin man with black hair and a five o'clock shadow he probably had to shave twice a day. He wore an old black cowboy hat that had some age on it and a long black duster. Under the brim of the hat his eyes were as hard as sapphires and about as warm. He walked slowly up to the bar and slammed a gold coin on the bar.

"Whiskey," he said, "and leave the bottle." His voice was cultured and educated, not the growl I was expecting. I picked up the coin and looked at it. It was real gold and rough around the edges. The coin was stamped with some kind of horror face on one side and two crossed swords on the other.

"Hey man, we don't take money for cosplay here", I said. I mean, where else would you get something like that right? He looked me dead in the eye with the emphasis on dead.

"That's a Demon Denarius, they're good anywhere." Again, I was impressed with the culture in his voice. It was almost soothing from such an intimidating figure. His hand struck out, snaking the coin from my fingers.

"This", and he held the coin up before my eyes, "is worth five bottles of whiskey Dave". My guts froze. How did he know my name? Like, seriously, the only other person who had known my name without me telling them was... Daniel. He slammed the coin back onto the bar.

"Now give me the bottle Dave...before I get... unpleasant". From the tone of his voice and his pauses, I figured unpleasant was his main emotion. He looked like the poster child for "Cowboys from Hell", and I took the coin slowly off the bar.

"So, do you need something for your horse too", I asked. I know, it wasn't smart but the gerbils had taken over once they stopped being frozen in fear. Yeah, ok, but if I was going to die, it was going to be as my true self, the smart ass who was too stupid to live.

I was staring at the man, waiting for him to decide my fate, when I heard a high pitched scream coming from my hand. I yelped and dropped the coin. Maybe I peed on myself a little and yes, maybe I sounded like a frightened ten year old watching a horror movie, but what else could I do? The coin continued screaming as it rattled to the bar.

The man roared with laughter as I leaped back from the coin on the bar. His whole body shook with mirth and he gasped for air. Hi, I'm Dave and welcome to my second mental breakdown. I looked at the coin on the bar and saw that it had landed face up. Even the face on the coin was contorted in laughter at my reaction. If I thought the owner of the bar had a sense of humor I would have been looking for cameras, sure that I was going to be the next fool on Funniest Videos International.

"I'm sorry, young sir", the man said, "but that joke never gets old". He then pulled a wad of cash from his pocket, peeled off two one hundred dollar bills and placed them on the bar. "For your trouble, and for the whiskey, barkeep."

Ok, so for that kinda tip, the guy could play all the pranks he wanted. I mean, who needs self respect, right? Not I, I thought to myself, and heard the tiny squeaky derisive laughter from my imaginary mental gerbils. I set the long necked bottle of whiskey on the bar.

"Three questions", I said. "One, how did you know my name, two what the hell is that coin, and three why did you have to pick this bar of all places?" The man poured a shot of whiskey and slammed it back.

"Young man, your name is written on your soul, right there on your chest. The Demon Denarius I brought back from my, vacation, though your description may be more accurate. And, I picked this bar as it is the last place to find who I am looking for."

"What's your name", I asked suspiciously. I had a bad feeling where this was going. Oh boy, did I have a bad feeling.

"My name is Hunter and I am... hunting... a customer of yours", he said with a contorted smile. Even the gerbils were frozen. This guy couldn't be the one Daniel had mentioned. I mean, Daniel wasn't real right? He was the product of my overworked mind. Or at least some really good drugs someone slipped me. None of that had really happened. It couldn't have. Hunter smiled again,

"Have you heard of me Dave", he asked. The shadows seemed to move around him like old friends as his voice grew lower. I felt trapped in the icy blue of his gaze, like a squirrel frozen in the truck's headlights right before there was a squeal, a thump, and it entered the squirrelly pearly gates.

I stood with my back firmly against the shelves full of bottles behind the bar. This wasn't happening again. Maybe I really was a resident at Grippy Socks Farms and I was on a bad trip. I mean maybe there were hot nurses? Couldn't I have hot nurses? With my luck they'd be from a horror video game, but a guy can dream right?

"There was a guy in here last week. He mentioned a man named Hunter, but you can't be him," I said.

"And why can't I be him, Dave", Hunter asked.

"Because none of that really happened", I kind of asked, hoping I was right.

"Don't worry Dave, I didn't believe I had met him either, right up until I woke up in Hell", Hunter said. "You know, dying isn't that bad, it's the coming back that's rough."

"I guess that gives a whole new meaning to 'unboxing video' huh", I asked without thinking. What was wrong with me? Here lies Dave. He died saying something sarcastic.

"Yes Dave, it really does", Hunter confirmed though I don't think he really got the reference. Which was probably good for me to be honest.

"So, woke up in Hell huh", I asked though I was sure I didn't want to know. See, this is how I get in trouble. I ask questions and people answer. Then monsters appear in the sky and I get slapped around like a hooker short twenty bucks. If there was a winner of the Darwin Awards, I would be Grand Champion.

"Yes, Dave, woke up in hell. Or, as I like to call it, my vacation".

"That's a hell of an idea of a vacation", I said. "So, how did that happen"?

"Do you really want to know Dave", he asked, "some people find the story... traumatic."

"Dude, I just pour drinks. If you want to talk you can. If not, you don't have to. I've learned to respect privacy in here", I said while gesturing vaguely around the bar. Customer service, thy name is Dave.

"No Dave, I will tell you. I will tell you and then... then you will tell *me* where Daniel is." I felt a warm menace deep in the cockles of my soul. Hehe... cockles. Never gets old, really.

"I was a normal enough man. Family, two kids, boring accounting job. I was your average middle American who never thought to much and never questioned my world. I went to the park on my lunch one day and sat down beside a stranger on a park bench. I really didn't want my ham sandwich, the same lunch everyday, so I began feeding the bread to the birds. The stranger started talking to me. Told me a strange story. I didn't believe it, but he was so very compelling. When he finished his story, I sat in silence for several moments. Before I could process his story the lake in front of us exploded. I could not understand what I was seeing. A... thing... erupted from the lake and attacked us. I saw an arm, something, coming at my head before some type of sucker or mouth attached to my head." Hunter stopped for a minute and slammed down another shot.

"I woke up in a strange place, like a desert with no wind. A desert on fire. I don't know how long I stumbled through that desert. Hours, weeks, months, I do not know. At some point I was attacked. I was beaten, tortured, brutalized is a good term. I had never been in a fight in my life. And I guess I still hadn't been since I was dead. But I fought there. I fought, I bled, I healed, I changed. Eventually I escaped. I have no idea how long I ran, the howling of their hounds chasing me, before I found a valley. In the center were standing stones, horrible spiked black glass and stone. Like the teeth of some long dead demon left in the sand. The hounds chased me into the center of the ring of stones. And, suddenly, I was back in my body, just being fed into the furnace of the crematorium. It must have been a shock for the guy in the funeral home when I started beating on the inside of the furnace to let me out". Hunter sat for a minute...brooding. He brooded so intensely it felt like meditation. Like the strength of his broodiness could tilt the universe. Hunter slowly reached out, poured another shot and drained it.

"Everything for the next few weeks is a blur", he continued. "I stumbled around back alleys, hiding, wondering when the hounds would find me. Finally, I was found, not by the hounds, but by a woman..." Feeling like I was sinking I interrupted him.

"Let me guess, she knew Daniel too?" I don't know why I felt compelled to say this, it just shot out of my mouth. Like so many times, my mouth was just living it's best life and damn the rest of me.

"Yes... she knew Daniel too", he said. "And like myself, her life had been horribly altered by such a meeting. Her name is Grace, and if you have not met her yet, you will soon Dave. She follows his trail like a thrall hoping to end her own torment".

"Geez dude, this is getting heavy. Like, can't you all just get along", I asked. He might kill me but dude, I didn't want to be dead and depressed. Guy really needed some happy in his life. Even undead happy or whatever. I could suddenly feel intensity roll off Hunter like it had weight. His face was hidden in shadow but his sapphire eyes glowed.

"Get along", he whispered. Then he thundered, "get along? Daniel is the reason I lost my life, my family, everything Dave. Have you ever had your head swallowed by a giant tentacle mouth Dave? Do you know how horrible that is", Hunter yelled at me. He was frothing at the mouth now. Literally frothing at the mouth.

"No but I think I saw that once on the internet, or something anyway", I said. Why did I say that? What was wrong with me? Dude was going to think I was a total perv.

I prayed he would let me clear my browser history before he killed me. Hunter stopped ranting immediately.

"That's gross Dave", he said, "like you have a problem, don't you?"

"It was one time at band camp ok", I said. Even the gerbils were on strike. They didn't want to be part of this conversation either.

"Wash your hands before you touch my glass next time", Hunter said with disgust in his voice.

"You're from Hell and you're giving me grief", I asked.

"There are limits Dave, even there", he said. He lifted his glass to take another shot, looked at it and put it back down.

"Let's get to the end of this shall we? here is Daniel?"

I started stammering, "he was in about a week ago and I'm not sure what happened. I saw things, things I don't understand. Then he was just gone."

"You saw things like you do on the internet Dave", he asked. I kinda felt like he was mocking me.

Grabbing every ounce of courage I had I said, "more like the roof came off and something giant and evil reached in here with about a hundred tentacles to fight Daniel. The last time I saw him, he was running out the door screaming at his 'dad'. I woke up on the floor a few minutes later like it never happened."

It was the truth. I couldn't believe it but I had lived it. It was like crystal dripping in my mind. I hadn't been able to face it until now, but it had really happened. I suddenly felt free, liberated, as if a weight had been lifted from me. Hunter stared at me as if he could see it. Like he could see it all click into place inside of me. He sat back slowly and tilted his hat back.

"I'm sorry Dave, I have misjudged you. It seems you are as much a prisoner here as I am".

"Prisoner", I asked, "what do you mean prisoner?" I was still in a foggy far off place processing the truth I had just realized. I knew it was all real and didn't know how to deal with knowing it. Yeah, it was confusing to me too. The walls of the bar shuddered once as though the building were giving off a warning. Hunter looked around for a minute.

"I've said too much and I will not be disrespectful. I need to leave before Daniel gets too far ahead." Hunter stood and simultaneously pulled his hat low on his head and slammed back a final shot. "Be careful Dave", he warned, "you are at the center of events far larger than you can imagine". Hunter turned and started towards the door as the walls shuddered again. I had never seen such a scary man move so fast. But I had never seen walls shudder like they were growling either. Just as he reached the door he turned back to me.

"Be careful Dave, all is not what it seems here. This is the start of this journey. You will see things, experience things you never have before. But do not forget what has come before". And with that cryptic soliloquy he turned and slid out of the bar. I don't know how long I stood motionless in the bar. I think it was Mickey moaning from the floor that brought me to my senses. What did he mean I was a prisoner here? What had come before? Even the gerbils in my head didn't have an answer for that one.

Sighing, I grabbed a mop from the closet at the back of the bar. I'd better mop up Mickey's blood, and probably other things, before someone pinned another nasty rag to the bar covered in whino piss this time. Where had that knife come from anyway?

I Met a Sleep Paralysis Demon

For those of you who may have missed my first couple of entries, my name's Dave and I'm the bartender at the Hellhound Bar. It's been a few weeks since Hunter left me with more questions than answers. Not much else has changed really. The patrons have continued their flaming dart competitions so now I have to replace the dart boards every few days. Last night Ryan and Short George got into an argument. It is kinda odd that Short George threw an axe at the dartboard but hey, I don't ask questions. Short George is a weird one anyway. You can't even see his face for all the beard and I swear I hear metal clanking every time he moves but I can barely see him over the bar, so who knows really. I just pour the drinks and clean up the mess. It's safer that way.

The other day the owner of the bar was waiting on me when I came in. He told me there had been complaints from the cleaning staff after closing. I told him I was tired of finding weapons pinned to my bar like psychotic love notes. The last one had been another knife pinning the mop to the closet door. How was I to know Mickey had done well, things in the corner of the bar? I mean, who does that? On the bright side, the girl from the Church of the Goldfish agreed to come by the bar sometime soon. I was really hoping she would.

I opened the bar and did my normal routine stocking and replacing everything that was needed for tonight's round of flaming debauchery. As I finished refilling the bin of paper umbrellas the door opened and in walked a small figure wearing a purple and pink puffer jacket and jeans with the hood up. Considering how crazy my last few afternoon patrons had been, I was glad there weren't tentacles or omens of imminent doom as he entered. I watched him out of the corner of my eye as he came up to the bar and had to do a little hop to get seated on the barstool. He wasn't short, just vertically challenged.

"What'll it be", I asked. I was truly hoping this was just a run of the mill dude down on his luck and wanting a quiet drink. I wasn't sure I could handle another incident.

"Rum, any rum, just rum", the stranger said as he pulled back his hood. I started to reach for the bottle then stopped. His skin was black, not like African American, black as tar. His eyes had red irises and his ears were slightly pointed. He grinned at me as I stood there with my mouth hanging open and I saw that his teeth were all sharp points.

"Yeah, yeah, you've never seen anyone like me. Now pour, please" he said. His voice had a high pitch to it. Not squeaky, but close. Taking a deep breath I asked the question burning in my mind.

"You don't know my name, do you"? I know, not what you were expecting right? His answer would be the deciding factor in whether I ran out of the bar screaming and never came back.

"How would I know your name", he asked. "I've never been here before . I relaxed with an audible sigh. Okay, so this was weird, but he wasn't a member of the Super Scary Weirdos Club like the last few afternoon customers. Shrugging I pulled down a bottle of rum and poured him two fingers in a glass.

"I'm sorry, things have been weird around here lately, I'm Dave and if you need anything else please let me know." I intended to slide him his drink and get back to whatever other chores needed doing around the bar.

Before I could take a step the little guy burst out with a squeaky, "do you know the worst thing about being a sleep paralysis demon?"

"A sleep what", I asked in confusion. Come on gerbils, help me out here I thought to myself.

"I'm Todd and I'm a sleep paralysis demon", the little guy said. He sat staring at the bar for a moment.

"I hate my job", he said in frustration and took a sip of his drink. I couldn't help but feel some sympathy for the guy. He looked so lost and sad. I mean yeah, he looked ferocious like he'd eat my liver with some beans, but he radiated such despair and hopelessness. Plus, he didn't give off an air of being willing to kill me on a whim, which I really appreciated.

"You sound like you could use a willing ear", I said. I don't know why I suddenly wanted to help the guy, I guess because I kinda felt the same way sometimes. Especially lately, the only positive to my day was visiting that strange little church and seeing... well, seeing her really.

"You wouldn't believe me if I told you", the little guy said dejectedly.

"Try me", I said laughing. After everything I had seen lately this should be a snap.

"Like I said, I'm a sleep paralysis demon and I hate my job". He started to perk up a little. "I mean, I never get any sleep, for one thing. Up all night doing my job, then double shifts for the people who sleep during the day, then just when I'm getting to sleep some telemarketer calls about my car warranty. Do I look like I drive a car Dave", he asked.

"Uhhhh...", I stumbled. I had no idea what to say. I need a warning label that reads "Warning: says stupid things when threatened." I just wasn't making much progress handling this one.

"You know, I've seen real evil Dave, but those people. Actually, I've always wondered if that wasn't a separate system of the Demonic Business Bureau. It's evil enough to be a pilot program from one of the big wigs."

"The what", I asked. That's it, I swear I'm evicting the gerbils. They were bloody useless these days. Must be on strike. Or maybe scared stupid, like I stayed these days.

"The DBB. Are you new here man? They control a lot of the local business ventures", he said.

"Is that who you work for", I asked.

"Me? No, I wish. They get benefits, vacations, even incentives. I get rooms full of flatulent bachelors. Do you know what it's like to squat on a guy's headboard for hours while he lets them rip in his sleep over and over. I swear one guy must have had a toxic waste dump in his guts. Another guy woke up swearing he'd never eat kielbasa again. There is no gas mask in any world that can help with that. And do you know the worst part", he asked.

"There's worse than that", I asked. I was a little mesmerized really.

"My clothes reek of farts when I go home. I mean reek. Like it's not bad enough to smell it there, I have to bring it home with me", he said. I stood there not knowing what to say. In the silence we heard snoring from one of the booths along the wall. I looked over, startled. How had Mickey gotten in here? I would have sworn he wasn't here when I opened. Todd looked over at the booth, then back at me.

"Would you like a little proof Dave", he asked. His whole face lit up with an evil grin and for a minute his whole personality changed. He was a new person, a brighter happier person, if overly malevolent in appearance. I smiled back. I didn't want anything bad to happen to Mickey but, well, he made every day miserable.

"Don't hurt him", I said. "He's a miserable old drunk but, still", I said.

"Don't worry Dave, I won't hurt him. We don't actually hurt people, just scare them a little." Todd hopped off his barstool and walked over to the booth. He climbed right up over the back of the booth and perched there. After a few seconds he held his hand over Mickey's head. There was a small flash and Todd was flung back into the booth behind him. Mickey farted and grunted loudly before rolling over on his side.

"What the hell was that", Todd yelled. "What the hell is he", Todd demanded pointing at Mickey.

"He's an old drunk who sneaks in here", I said confused. This situation was just getting stranger. I needed a sign over my head reading "confused". It could be pink and purple neon and blink. With my luck it would be half burned out but hey. Blowing on his still sizzling palm Todd stumbled back to the bar.

"I've been doing this for three thousand years, without a vacation mind you, and never had that happen. Whatever you think he is Dave, you're very wrong", Todd said as he hopped back up onto the barstool and shook his head.

"Pour me another, will ya", he asked in his squeaky voice. I poured him another two fingers and he sipped it slowly, relishing the alcohol as it entered his system.

"See, it's stuff like that", he said disgustedly. "Can't a simple guy make a living? I just shook my head. I was sure this would make sense in bizarro world but I was absolutely lost in the situation. Most of our patrons at least looked moderately normal. Well, except for Christo, but I'm sure all that slime was just a skin condition. But this little guy was just different. I had somehow stepped to the left again and ended up doing the inter-dimensional hokey pokey.

Before Todd could notice my fugue we both heard a ringing. It was a cell phone. Todd and I both froze. A look of sheer horror passed over his face. Todd reached into his pocket and slowly drew out a small purple cell phone. His movements had a nightmarish quality like time had slowed and the air was made of molasses. Flipping open the phone, Todd answered it.

"Hello", Todd squeaked into the tiny phone. Todd got smaller and smaller, huddling into his puffer jacket. An interrupted stream of "yes, sir", and "of course, sir", was all he was able to mumble into the phone. Finally, he closed it dejectedly and stood looking at it. Poor dude was all huddled up like a kicked puppy.

"Hey man, you ok", I asked after a few seconds.

"That was my boss, Mr. Williams", Todd said, then released a long hissing sigh of frustration. I noticed his small pink tongue was forked as it flickered out of his mouth and back in.

"If you don't want to talk about it, that's ok", I said and poured him more rum. It was obvious he needed something. I could barely see him standing at the bar he had shrunk so much.

"My boss is a real asshole", Todd said and sucked the rum down. He started to perk up a little.

"I mean, okay he's a demon, but that's no reason to treat us like crap is it", Todd asked. "We should be treated with respect like anyone else.". Todd was obviously letting the alcohol affect him.

"But aren't demons supposed to be kinda assholish", I asked. Would it be a shock to you to know I was confused? I mean, even the gerbils were holding up question mark signs.

"No", Todd slurred, "demons might just be the best people. My poor blighted mother was the kindest evil entity you could have ever asked to meet really." Todd flung his left arm up in a grand gesture.

"Always ready to flay a human or lead a small pack of wolves to a village was my mom", Todd said proudly. "But, Mr. Williams", he continued, "all he cares about is numbers. How many people did I paralyze and do I have receipts for my expense account".

"We're demons, Dave, demons. And he's worried about data tables and spreadsheets", Todd continued. He was obviously warming to his topic. "What happened to the good old days of pestilence and despair", Todd demanded. "What happened to sacrifices and dancing naked with witches around fires?" Todd suddenly looked at me and squinted.

"Are there any witches around here Dave", he asked slushily.

"Witches", I asked. Yes, I know my mother dropped me on the head a lot. I pour drinks and mop spills. Whitty conversation is so not what I was hired for.

"Yes, witches, Dave", Todd said with a leer and a grin. "Some of those witches are sexy as hell, even if most of them wouldn't give my kind the time of day." He suddenly looked dejected again.

"Why wouldn't they", I asked. I was honestly interested. I mean, if I was going to the rubber room palace I might as well know the answer, right?

"Most witches are actually good, Dave", he said. "It's only a few that actually mess with demons like me. But a demon can dream can't he", he asked and tried to wink at me.

The surreal nature of a demon attempting to wink and leer at me was just too much. I just had to like the little guy. Okay, so he might be a sleep paralysis demon, but he seemed a good sort and was funny. Everyone has bad things about them. That doesn't make them bad people, right? I mean, right?

As I pondered this philosophical question, we both heard a groan and a shuffle as Mickey sat up slowly from the booth. The smell of stale alcohol and staler urine wafted towards us. Todd and I made eye contact for a second, frozen in a kind of abject terror. Before I could say anything, Todd had thrown two silver coins on the bar and hopped to the floor from his barstool.

"Thanks for everything, Dave", he squeaked in a rush as he sprinted towards the door and almost through it. Mickey obviously terrified him, but why? He was just an old drunk.

I looked at the coins on the bar and then back at Mickey. He was grinning beatifically. Looking at his feet, I inwardly screamed. He had pissed himself again and left a puddle in the floor. Looking back up at his face I saw a glow about his eyes before they rolled back up in his head and he slumped backwards into the booth. Bastard didn't even have the decency to hit his head on the way down either.

Shrugging in bewilderment, I turned to the broom closet to get a mop. As I opened the closet, I heard a soft pop. Mickey was gone. Just gone, vanished into thin air. What the hell? He had just passed back out. Where could he have vanished to? Grabbing the mop I went to the booth. He wasn't under it either. The only sign he had been there was the smell and the puddle. I shook my head and started mopping. This place just got weirder by the day.

Tim the Cursed

My name's Dave and I'm the bartender here at the Hellhound Bar. Hopefully by now you've heard some of my stories and now you're back for more. This next story's a little different so I hope you'll hold on with me. This was a change of pace for the bar. Of all the crazy things I've seen this one guy just broke my heart.

It was another quiet lonely day in the bar. Wanda had wandered in for a few minutes looking for a hook up before storming out while hiking up her leopard skin skirt. I really hoped what I had seen under it had been underwear. Please let it have been underwear!

Other than that, the day seemed normal. Come to think of it, every day seems like every other really. The only difference seems to be the chaos the patrons bring with them. This day was different. I had just finished bringing up supplies from the basement when the front door opened. I looked up in dread, wondering what nightmarish hell monster was coming in now. But it wasn't, at least not at first glance.

In walked an average dude. Six foot or so, normal beard, blonde hair and dressed in a rather dapper suit. He walked up to the bar and sat staring into the mirror behind the bar. That mirror creeped me out honestly. Sometimes it seemed like the reflection moved on it's own. Or maybe things were looking back out at you, who knew?

I walked over and asked, "what'll you have"?

"Vodka, if you have it", he responded. His voice was normal with a deep southern twang to it. That rolling country sound you could only get if you lived there all your life. As distinctive as a Bostonians in it's own way.

"One Vodka coming up", I said retrieving a bottle from behind the bar and pouring for him. I was just so glad to have a normal customer for once. I was all but giddy to not have to be in fear for my life or my soul. It was refreshing to not feel existential dread or the doom of the universe while pouring a drink. The blonde man stared at the shot for a minute before gently picking it up and throwing it back.

"Thank you sir, may I please have another", the man asked.

"Sure", I said and poured a second shot. I managed not to comment on the loose David Copperfeild reference that floated through my mind. Maybe I was getting smarter? Nah! He picked it up and then looked me in the eyes. Huh, dude had normal eyes too. Today was my lucky day!

"So, what's your name", I asked. I had to admit I was kind of excited. I was finally going to get to talk to a normal human. It had been a while between tentacle men, cursed hunters, demons and whatever the owner was.

"I'm Tim, and you are", he inquired.

"My name's Dave and I bartend here", I said before realizing I sounded like a moron again. That was really a bad habit, why did I do that? Was I campaigning for village idiot?

"I can see that", he said with a laugh, "and I'm a grateful soul." The man reached into his pocket and pulled out a few gold coins and a red velvet bag. He placed two coins on the bar and asked, "will you please keep them coming"?

"Sure", I said, probably sounding like a happy puppy. "So, what's in the bag", I asked.

"Hhhmmmmm", he mumbled inquisitively. His mouth was full of vodka again.

"The red velvet bag you had with the coins", I explained. He looked confused for a moment before pulling the bag back out of his pocket and holding it up for me to see.

"This is what's known as a mojo hand, though really it's a gris gris", he said rather quietly. Why did I feel like this conversation was about to go bad?

"Gris gris are charms mostly. For luck or love or other things", he continued. "But this one is special."

"What makes it special", I asked. I didn't want to know, I really didn't want to know. Damnit, he was supposed to be normal like me. Wait, was I normal? Before I could think about that he continued.

"This doesn't contain a charm, this contains my curse", he said Just kinda deadpan he talked about being cursed. Like it was an everyday occurrence.

"Your curse", I stammered. Damnit, damnit, the guy wasn't normal after all. Why me? What terror or horrible death would this guy bring into my life? Tentacles weren't enough?

"I'm known as Tim, the Cursed One", he said flatly. "You see I loved the wrong woman, and when she destroyed me I sought an end to the pain. But instead, things worked out in another way". Tim rocketed back another shot of vodka before placing the shot glass back on the bar. I sighed heavily.

"Fine, just fine", I said, suddenly defeated. I drug a small stool over and perched behind the bar to listen. Normal was too much to hope for and the gerbils in my head were hardened at this point, so I might as well listen. The owner hated the stool but I didn't care anymore. I'd almost died or went mad too many times.

"Lay it on me", I said with a sigh. Tim looked at me for a moment, fiddling with the bag and downing another shot.

"A few years ago I was in love with this girl named Allie. She wasn't particularly attractive, but I thought she was a good woman and I tried to love her and make her happy. She was the horribly jealous type and anytime a woman even looked in my direction she would make my life hell. She would constantly accuse me of cheating and lying. After about four years she dumped me. I found out later she dumped me on the way to see the man she had been cheating on me with for months. I was devastated, just broken. Even after we broke up she continued to harass me. She ruined my birthday standing in my front yard screaming at me that I was a liar and a cheater. The last straw was when she broke into my house and tried to sexually assault me while I was sleeping. I just couldn't take it anymore so I went to see a friend who was a witch". He paused here and laid the bag on the bar, staring at it without seeing it.

"Man, that's rough", I said and honestly felt for the guy. The whole conversation obviously caused him a lot of pain. No one ever believed men could be abused too. I was abused daily in this bar but at least my abusers weren't anyone I loved. Feared maybe, but not loved. Tim looked up at me with the lopsided grin of the somewhat insane.

"Oh, wait, it gets so much better", he said. I didn't like the way that sounded. "I begged the witch to just help me let Allie go. To just stop hurting. The witch gave me a piece of paper, a satchet of herbs and a pen. She told me to write Allie's name three times on the paper then throw the paper and the herbs in the fire. That was it, just throw it in and the pain would end. I did it, but it didn't work out that way", he paused again here. I hadn't filled up the shot glass and he was waiting patiently. I hastily poured the shot so he would continue. I was invested damnit.

"As soon as the paper and herbs hit the fire things in me changed. I didn't feel the pain of Allie's loss anymore. But in front of me stood a ghost, a specter of Allie silently screaming at me. The old witch took ashes from the fire and scraped them into the red bag. She told me that until I found true love the specter of Allie would follow me, constantly screaming, to remind me of my pain and being separate from it". He stopped here and silence filled the bar. I really didn't want to ask it but I just had to know. I'm really stupid sometimes.

"So why not just yeet the bag", I asked. "Get rid of it."

"Yeet", he mocked, "such a strange word". He shook his head and had another shot. He'd drained most of the bottle.

"I've tried throwing it away, burning it, burying it. It always ends up back in my pocket. It follows me no matter what I do." Having said this, he picked the bag up off the bar and put it back in his pocket.

"So, is she like here now", I asked, looking around in confusion.

"She's right behind you Dave", he said softly. I yelped and jumped off the stool. I whacked my knee on the bar and stumbled around on one foot frantically searching the bar for the ghost. Tim was trying not to laugh. Or at least I think he was. It's hard to tell when you've manually tried to remove your own kneecap. He pointed to the mirror behind the bar.

"She's in the mirror Dave", he said. "She's in every mirror or any glass that gives a reflection". He downed the last shot, having killed the bottle. "My abuser torments me for all time, and I can never be free".

"That really sucks", I moaned, not sure if I felt more for him or for my kneecap. "I'm sorry", I said to him as he turned to leave. He stopped for a minute.

"It could be worse", he said and I felt cold inside. Here it was, here's where I finally died. He told me all this and now can't leave witnesses. I knew it. Hail the Mighty Goldfish, to whom I commend my soul in the Eternal Fishbowl I thought to myself. Tim suddenly smiled.

"Have you met the guy with the tentacle porn 'stache Dave", he asked.

"It could always be worse", and with that he laughed and walked out the door. I sat there for a while, rubbing my aching kneecap, and wondering what anyone could ever do to deserve that?

Necro Business

Hi, it's me again. Dave from The Hellhound Bar. And wow do I have another story for you. This one was very different for me so you'll just have to hear it and you can judge. For myself, I'm kind of becoming numb to the weirdness factor. I mean, tentacles, demons, hunters, my boss; they just all kind of become one great woobie of weirdness and I and the fearless gerbils just can't keep up anymore. There's a limit to what a simple bartender can deal with.

The owner of the bar has been having these strange meetings in the back room. He warned me, very politely, not to come to the back room no matter what. But then these strangers come in randomly, totally hooded and cloaked so that I can't even see their eyes. The robes or cloaks or whatever don't even fit right. They're shaped oddly or have pieces that shouldn't fit. I don't know what to do except to pretend not to notice. Probably safer that way.

On the bright side, I went to my first bake sale for the Church of the Goldfish. To be honest, I went to see if I could find her, but it was still a bake sale. There were some really strange items there too. Eyelid cake, Finger Mousse, Cream of the Old Gods. Not really sure what that's about but, you guessed it, she was there. Her name's Liz and she may be the prettiest woman I've ever met. No, really, at least I think so anyway. She showed me around the little church, the alter holding a small crystal goldfish in a bowl. It glowed with purple light. She even showed me some of the forbidden murals. Paintings of the Great Goldfish swimming through emptiness and creating the universe with a swipe of it's tail fin. It's a strange religion, but no stranger than any other. I mean, there's that cult of the followers of the Demented Fistula down the street and they're really weird.

Anyway, back to the story. I was standing bored behind the bar last Friday afternoon. At least, I think it was Friday. Time is just different here. Everything had been stocked, the fire extinguishers were ready in case of another flaming dart tournament, and I was slowly building a real case of existential dread for the evening to come. The same as any other Friday really. As the gerbils were getting up to a more fevered pitch over "how was Dave going to die tonight", I heard the little bell above the bar door tinkle.

I looked over to see a simple man, brown hair, clean shaven in khakis and a simple polo walk in. It was the kind of outfit that screamed middle management. The guy walked erect like he was confident, but I could tell by the set of his shoulders and the slight downward tilt of his head that he was worn down. This was a guy who had been beaten down by life and was just getting through one energy drink at a time. I wondered if he worked in retail. Now, there's a job full of existential dread and the urge to die.

Mr. Middle Management casually walked up to the bar and took a seat. I could tell he was trying to scope the place out without looking like that's what he was doing. As this was not unusual in a bar full of nothing but odd behavior and odder (ahem) people, it didn't worry me. The gerbils lay snoozing in my imaginary mind, so it couldn't mean trouble, right?

I walked over to him and asked, "what'll you have", in my most customer service oriented voice. It probably didn't sound all that friendly but hey, it's the effort right?

"I'd like an Old Fashioned please", he said.

"Bourbon", I asked. It was traditional, but with people nowadays I had to ask.

"Oh, yeah, please", the guy said. I think I startled him with the question. He wass out of sorts. Maybe his gerbils and my gerbils were family? Who knew?

"Classy", I said, "coming right up". And it was a rather classy drink. Versions of the Old Fashioned were being tried by bartenders as early as the prohibition Era in America.

"So, what brings you in", I asked as I laid out the sugar, bitters, and bourbon to make the cocktail.

"I'm trying to avoid my family right now", he said while looking down at the bar.

"Not big drinkers, huh", I asked.

"Huh", he replied. I felt he was a kindred spirit at that moment. Huh was an inherent part of both our languages. Kinda made me feel warm and fuzzy inside.

"Your family, they're not big drinkers", I asked. "Since you're hiding in a bar and all."

"Oh", he said charmingly and looked like he was trying to catch up on the conversation. Dude was definitely a long lost cousin. Had to be. If not in body, at least in spirit.

"No, not really what I meant", he said and looked uncomfortable. "You see, my family is really powerful and they've been hounding me for years to come back to the family business and it's just not a life I want."

"Hey, a life with money can't be all that bad, right", I asked and gestured vaguely at myself. I didn't really mean to say I was poor but let's be real, I didn't work here for the thrills. As a matter of fact, why did I work here again?

"Money", he asked. Oh, but he was elegant in his speech. It was beautiful.

"Money means powerful doesn't it", I asked. I was starting to think we were having two different conversations.

"Oh, they have money, but it's their power that scares me," he said and sipped his drink.

"They must be politicians", I said wisely. That's me, your local detective behind the bar. A sage really. Intelligence with a capital I.

"They're necromancers Dave", he said flatly. "They raise the dead for money. It really is a noble profession, but I want to be normal", he sighed in disgust.

Oh shit, I thought in panic. He knew my name. Oh shit, I was going to die. I hadn't told him my name. Oh god, would it be tentacles again? The gerbils were awake and preparing to abandon ship. Or would that be, abandon Dave?

"How did you know my name", I asked. I was shaking, terrified.

"Uh, it's on your nametag man", he said looking at me like I had lost my mind. Technically I had. I looked down at my shirt, just remembering that the owner had given me a nametag. Who had ever seen a bartender with a nametag? I mean, really?

"You Dave, me Kevin", he said in a sad caveman imitation. I stood there, feeling stupid for a minute. I don't think I drooled on myself. Then the conversation caught up to me. Did he say necromancers?

"Did you say necromancers", I asked.

"Are you feeling ok", he asked while staring at me. "I can go", he said and started to get up.

"No, no", I said and waved him to sit back down. "Sorry, it just tripped me up for a second."

"Ok", he said and sat cautiously back down. But I could tell he wasn't sure if he should. I could see that internet review, "come have drinks with the craziest bartender you'll ever meet. He can make you uncomfortable with just a sentence."

"I'm sorry, I just had this really strange customer. It kinda scarred me", I tried to explain.

"Oh, I guess that makes sense", he said and relaxed.

"Did you say necromancers", I asked again. I mean, I tried, I really tried to let it go ok? I know, I disappoint me to sometimes.

"Yeah, necromancers. My family is the last family of necromancers alive", he said. He looked me dead in the eye, pun intended, as he said it too. Dude wasn't joking.

"Like D&D", I asked hopefully.

"No Dave", he said and sighed again. "Like zombies and crawling body parts and the spirits of the dead kind of necromancers."

"Uh", I said. See, we had to be cousins. Well, in spirit at least.

"My whole life was raise this zombie, make that heart beat outside the guys chest", he continued. "My family pet was an animated segment of intestines that squiggled behind me everywhere like a slimy snake. When I asked for a dog instead my father handed me a shovel and told me to go dig one up."

"Intestines", I gulped. My mind was overtaken by the image of a friendly writhing mass of intestines nuzzling at a young boy's feet while he did homework. Oh, that was gross. Oh, worse thought, what did that smell like?

"When I was a kid my nanny was a zombie. I really liked her but pieces kept falling off. I remember laying in my bed and finding her fingers under the sheets touching me", he said with a smile. Like this was a pleasant memory or something.

"Ugh", I said before I could help it. This guy was a walking book of trauma if that's what he had happy memories about.

"Anyway, so I decided black robes and body parts just weren't for me you know", he asked. "I left, went to college, tried to be normal", he went on. "Do you know how hard it is to be normal when roadkill accidentally shows up at the door to your dorm at three a.m." he asked.

"Guess that makes it hard to feel normal huh", I asked.

"They didn't tell me that if I didn't use my power it would find a way to work without me", he said. "No one bothered to mention that driving by a cemetery on a date would result in zombies following me to my girlfriend's house just as we were getting naked."

"Well, if she had a zombie fetish", I started then shut up. Hey, it's a thing. I mean, I wouldn't know. I heard about it once, ok?

"Oh dude", he said with a look of sick horror. "You're not one of those zombie groupies are you?"

"The kind that follow murder mystery shows and fantasizes about being murdered", he asked.

"That's a thing", I asked, my eyes widening in shock.

"That's the tame version", he said and laughed.

"I really don't want to know" I said. Oh please, I did not want to know.

"All through college my family wanted me to settle down and start having kids. Maybe build a small castle near a large cemetery or something. Like that was my dream, a wife, two kids, a moat, and a zombie named spot", he said.

"So, what did you do", I asked. Look, I was invested ok. The gerbils were holding up mental signs reading "turn back now" but I just couldn't.

"I got a job. Human Resources Manager for a large business firm. I figured Human Resources was a pit of evil and despair so I would fit right in", he explained.

"Yeah, it does seem that way", I said thinking back to my own days in the corporate world. Honestly, he didn't seem evil enough for Human Resources. I mean, don't you have to have a personal letter from a greater demon to work in that field?

"It was great", he said with the first real enthusiasm he had shown. "I mean, there were no burning coals or barbed wire whips, but it was a good job. I didn't really like how my boss enjoyed torturing the employees mentally and financially, but hey, he was the boss", he said and shrugged.

"Yeah, I guess that could be a problem", I said wisely. I didn't understand what he was talking about really, but hey, when in doubt make it look like you know what's going on. At least, that's how I did it. No wonder I work here.

"It was all going well. My family didn't have a clue where I was at and I was starting to get noticed, right", he said, clearly expecting me to agree.

"Sure", I mumbled. I wasn't sure at all, but maybe if I agreed with him enough he'd tip well?

"Then, one day last week, my boss has a heart attack at the weekly staff meeting", he said. "I didn't think anything about it. I just started doing CPR. It had been so long since my power cut loose", he said and shook his head.

"Oh, no", I said, dreading what came next.

"One second he was purple and stone dead. The next he had jumped up and bitten his receptionist right on the ass". I busted out laughing. I couldn't help it.

"That's a new definition for sexual harassment", I said and snorted.

"It's not funny Dave", he said. "He bit a huge portion out of her ass and she almost bled to death".

"Was she hot", I asked innocently. Hey, I mean, you know I could understand if she was cute and all.

"Ugh, no Dave", he said with a shiver. "She was sixty and about four hundred pounds. Honestly, if he hadn't been a zombie he would have never been able to chew through the granny panties", he said and started laughing himself. The mental image was just too horrifying. To die, become a zombie, then have to bite through granny panties? That's its own hell.

"So, they fired me, saying I caused the issue", he went on. "Nevermind that they had no idea of what I was. I was just the scapegoat. And do you know what's worse", he asked. The gerbils were screaming at me not to make a smart alec remark. But do I listen?

"He had shitty breath", I asked.

"The next day I hear a knock at my apartment door", he said, obviously not hearing my comment in the retelling of his story. "My whole family was waiting in the hallway dressed in their black robes with their incense and chanting. They had even brought one of the girls from the local village. While I had been gone they had been grooming her to be my wife."

"Was she, you know, alive", I asked. It was sick I know but, inquiring minds need to know these things.

"What", he asked in shock and stared at me.

"Well, I mean, I didn't know", I stumbled.

"Of course she was alive Dave", he said in disgust. "Just because we raise the dead doesn't mean we mate with them. I mean, no matter what Uncle Leroy says", he said then trailed off blushing furiously.

I let that one go. All of you would have been so proud of me, even the gerbils did a happy dance. For once I didn't give in. I gave myself a little pat on the back. Okay, I lasted for three seconds.

"So, no cold packing huh", I asked. He had just taken the last sip of his old fashioned and choked. Coughing furiously, he was obviously trying not to choke to death.

"Dude, that's gross", he wheezed before devolving into fits of laughter.

"You're a sick man, Dave, but I like it. Thank you, I needed that", he said and slowly stood to leave.

As he walked towards the door I said, "Stop by sometime, let me know how it works out." He turned back to look at me and his eyes glowed with a black fire.

"Oh, you'll see me again Dave, don't worry. Maybe I'll invite you to the wedding". And with that he left. I didn't know whether to be excited or scared really. I mean, they always say to beware the zombie raiser's, right?

Gurk

To quote the stupid human, my name is Gurk and I work at the Hellhound Bar. See, if the stupid human can do it, so can I. The man left his device at the bar tonight as he left. He was so interested in trying to go meet the Priestess at the Holy Temple he abandoned his device. Stupid human. He does not see this as our fierce god's temple, no he does not. Stupid human does not see how everything he does reflects on our Master.

No, he sits and whimpers over the Priestess, then he whimpers in fear, and then he whimpers about cleaning. He should feel honored to clean these floors, but no, he leaves it all to us. Messages Gurk has left him. And when he did not see the messages, too stupid was he, we left threats. If he continues, we will talk to the Master about letting us kill him as a more permanent message. We are not his maids......we are the Master's.

Gurk was peaceful once. All were until the tentacle in the sky destroyed our world. We became warriors to fight the tentacle thing and save our people. Gurk's whole family died fighting, except Gurk's sister. But Gurk fought on, built a tribe to continue to fight. Years went on and all fought, but our world was lost. We, Gurk's tribe, are all that remain of The People. We were saved by the Master and brought here. We serve Him, not the stupid human. Where does the Master find these beings anyway? The stupid human writes many words on here. Words that go into the Diverse Dimensions, but he does not know this. If the Master knows, he does not stop it.

Gurk and his people clean the temple every night. We straighten the chairs, mop, and do all the repairs of what was destroyed the night before. Chairs and tables get smashed, Gurk and his people fix. Dart boards set on fire, we fix. Ugh, why is this language so hard? Gurk is great teacher in his own language, but in this Gurk sounds like imbecile. Stupid translator.

Master has spoken with me about stupid human several times. The other week the stupid human left a mess on the floor. Gurk's sister cleaned it up with no problem. Sister thinks stupid human is cute. Wants to lay with him. Gurk left stupid human a message with Gurk's second best knife. Gurk's second best! And the stupid human complains! It was an insult to Gurk and all Gurk's ancestors! Stupid human makes so many mistakes.

Today the Priestess came to see him. She looked softer, younger to Gurk. She walked in wearing her golden robes of office. Stupid human drooled and stared instead of bowing low. She is ancient, as old as her Great Goldfish, and he stood drooling like she was to be mated. We watched, we always watch, but he does not see us. Maybe the stupid human does not know who she is, or what she means to the Master? If the Master finds out, stupid human will die badly. Master and the Priestess.....well, never mind, not Gurks place.

Gurk tries to never speak ill of the Master. If it was not for the Master, Gurks entire race would be gone. But the Master plays dangerous games. He is assembling the forces of old.

Gurk knows the Demonic Business Bureau goes too far, but our tiny dimension cannot withstand a war. Gurk is scared, scared for his people and scared for himself. If the Master is killed, Gurks people will die as well. Gurk's life here is not great, but better than being dead.

Gurk must go clean up. Short George the Dwarven Lord has smashed all the tables because someone couldn't tell that she was married by the rings woven into her beard. Mickey, the oldest, has left another offering of wisdom on the floor to become the rain that brings growth to another dimension. It is a shame the stupid human does not know what Mickey really is. The stupid human is blind.

Yesterday the stupid human entered the temple, turned on all the lights, and almost stepped on Gurk. Gurk was just dusting the chairs, but the stupid human never sees. He thinks we don't see what he watches on this device either. The stupid human has interesting tastes. Gurk does not know what hentai is, but it sounds like food.

Gurk is sure the stupid human will leave more messes for Gurk, but this is Gurk's purpose. Gurk hopes the stupid human survives dealing with the Priestess, or the Master, or Short George, or Gurk's sister. Gurk must go now, much to do to clean the temple.

Barista Vision

It's me again everyone, um Dave, I mean. I'd love to tell you all about the last few days here at the bar but I'm really freaking out here. I came in yesterday and someone else had been on my laptop. Yeah, ok, so I shouldn't have left it at work but I didn't think anyone would mess with it. I feel so, violated. Someone calling themselves "Gurk" got access to all my files and even published a story on here for all of you to see. It wasn't even well written, just drivel. Not that I'm an expert or anything but come on.

Anyway, I've got my laptop on lockdown now and I've been watching. I hate to say this, but the story makes sense. The only way this place stays clean and repaired would be for some magical race of fairies or goblins to be doing the cleaning after I close every night. And considering everything else I've seen here, is it really that strange a concept? Tentacle people, hunters, demons, and necromancers have all drank at this bar. So why not invisible hyper violent cleaning staff? Who knew they'd be so stabby?

I opened about twenty minutes ago and did my pre opening walkthrough for invisible murder janitors with still no results. Liz, my um, girlfriend, was due to stop by in a few minutes. Ok, so maybe "girlfriend" is too broad a term, but I was hopeful! God, I'm such a schmuck. She's just so beautiful and innocent. Like all the goodness in the universe shines out through her eyes. Call me a simp if you want, it's still how I feel. Whatever. Anyway, she should be here any minute.

I got the chairs down stacked and the ice stocked behind the bar before I heard the bell above the door give its tinkle. I had been searching for the mop for the last few minutes and I couldn't find it anywhere. Mickey must have been in the bar recently.

I froze for a second, the gerbils holding their breath. I wasn't sure whether I was more afraid it was Liz or some eldritch being of madness and decay jonesing for some liquid anesthesia. Both seemed equally terrifying at that moment. The gerbils mocked my fear as I turned slowly towards the door. And saw the greatest vision of beauty the universe could bestow. All I could see was the light from the door granting her beauty a halo of goodness as she graced the bar with her gentle presence. It was a moment worthy of an eighties movie montage, even with the gerbils making gagging sounds in the echoes of my addled mind.

"Dave, are you ok", she asked as she walked in. Her chestnut hair fell perfectly around her shoulders and framed her face with character and peace. She had such delicious curves hinted at but mostly hidden under her robes. Her dark green eyes held a world of light and glowed with her inner joy.

"Dave", she said in a more concerned tone. Her voice was like the gentle sounds of doves on the wind. Oh god, I needed to answer her!

"I'm ok", I croaked and tried again. "Sorry, yeah I'm good, I just can't seem to find the mop", I wheezed and tried to laugh a little. Sir Putz-a-Lot at your service madam. Geeky and awkward is my specialty.

"You're cute when you're startled", she said and walked towards me.

"I'm cute", I asked dazedly. She thought I was cute! This wasn't happening. She giggled.

"Of course, silly, and I brought you a muffin", she said excitedly. I just noticed she had been carrying an oversized muffin in her hand.

"It's blueberry, that is what you like right", she asked.

"Yeah", I stammered, "but how did you know that?"

"Oh, I pay attention Dave, to everything about you", she smiled as she said it.

"This is really good", I mumbled through bites of the muffin. The wrapper had some kind of ball or something as its logo. I always skipped breakfast and I was starving.

"Where did you get this", I asked. It was delicious.

"There's a new coffee shop down the street", she said and sat in one of the chairs. She motioned for me to sit as well. I sat without thinking. The muffin was so good!

"It's called 'Oracle Dreams' and it has some great stuff. I saw the muffins on the way here and I knew you hadn't eaten", she said and looked down for a moment. She seemed almost shy.

"Th-thank you", I stammered. That was the nicest thing anyone had done for me in a while. I was blushing but I couldn't look away from her. I felt entranced, I couldn't not look at her. It was like a compulsion. But if I were to die, there were many more horrible ways than staring adoringly at Liz as I munched a muffin. I mean, Ok I didn't mean that the way it sounded. Or read, anyway, moving on.

"That was really nice", I mumbled. Ok, so I was embarrassed, but she was beautiful and funny and I was just some idiot bartender who worked too much and had a penchant for letting his mouth try to get him killed. She just seemed way out of my league. Guys like me never get the girl, we barely get to live.

"Oh, I'd do just about anything for you Dave", she said and leaned towards me.

My mind fixated on visions of what anything could be but for once, my mouth remained closed. All praise the Goldfish! Wait! She was leaning towards me. Were we finally going to, you know, kiss? And where was that giggling coming from?

I sat stunned as she moved closer. I mean, sure I'd kissed girls before. Lots of times really. Really. But this was, this was Liz! Our lips were so close to touching I could feel her breath on my face. Almost.

The little bell on top of the door gave its happy little jingle and Liz sprang back from me. She was breathing heavily and wouldn't look at me as the intruder, I mean a customer came in.

"Hi," an overly cheerful voice chimed into the bar. "Anyone here?"

Liz hurriedly backed away from the table, and from me, as the dreadfully cheerful person entered. Liz looked startled, almost frightened.

"Hi", the young girl said as she saw us. "I'm Sydney, like Sydney Australia", she said and giggled. Yes, she actually giggled. Uugh.

She was maybe five foot four and looked to be of Asian descent. Short black hair and a yellow jacket covering blue jeans completed the look of superb cheerfulness. Was this what ultimate evil looked like? Liz looked at the specter of cheerfulness and then back at me.

"Um, I'm sorry, I've got to go", she said and started for the door.

"Wait, I brought coffee", Sydney like Sydney Australia said. Sure enough she was carrying four cups of what smelled like a divine holy substance. I was convinced coffee was what they were talking about when ancient myths described mana or ambrosia.

"Coffee", I said hopefully. The gerbils took over for a minute sniffing the air. Little caffeine addicted furry monsters, all of them.

"No, really", Liz muttered as she sprinted out the door.

Great, I was so close to a kiss. Finally, a kiss with a real girl. The girl of my dreams. I mean I've kissed girls before. I have!

I turned to Sydney and she was watching the contrail from Liz's departure. She turned back to me with a quizzical expression on her face before lighting me up with the Jumbotron 3000 smile again. Damned thing could have blinded the sun.

"So, I brought coffee and some snacks from my new shop". Happiness pulsed from her in waves. But, there were snacks. Surely anyone bringing snacks and coffee couldn't be completely evil. I stopped and looked closer. Nope, her eyes weren't glowing either. I breathed a sigh of relief.

"Well, I mean, thanks", I mumbled. "But the you still you meant to bring that, well, here?"

"Of course", she giggled again. "My Gran and I just opened our coffee shop down the lane and we thought it would be a great idea to bring samples to some of the other businesses. You know, goodwill and all that", her sentence kind of drifted off. It may have had something to do with the look of utter confusion on my face. Goodwill? Coffee shop? Come on gerbils, don't fail me now.

"Oh, I thought one of the holy women had been in the shop earlier", she said as she drifted closer. For a moment she seemed confused.

"Huh", I asked. Loquacious as always, yep that's me.

"The wrapper on the table", she said, coming to stand in front of me. "That's from our shop", she said and held up a similarly wrapped item with a little crystal ball logo on the wrapper. It was another muffin like the one Liz had given me.

"Oh yeah, Liz brought that for me", I said kind of dumbly. Ok, so I wasn't the greatest at talking to pretty girls. I wasn't intimidated or anything, just hadn't had a lot of practice.

"Strange", Sydney said, "I could have sworn the lady earlier was way older but, like whatever." She lit me up with another sun scorching smile.

"Maybe it was someone else from the temple", I said. Liz was young so of course it was someone else. Like, duh. Oh man, now I was doing it.

"Of course", she burbled. "You know, you're kind of cute".

"Huh", I said again. No one had ever told me I was cute before. Like I said, just a lack of practice right?

"Was that your girlfriend", Sydney asked.

"Liz, yeah, I guess you could say that", I replied. I wasn't blushing, I wasn't. Damnit Dave, stop looking at your feet. I looked back up at her.

"Too bad", she said and giggled. "But, like anyway our shop is called Oracle Dreams and we make the best coffees and sweets this side of the multiverse", she said and handed me a cup of coffee.

Since I was trying to appear suave and debonair and not say a single thing to make me look as stupid as I felt, I took a sip of the coffee. And moaned. It was what life must have been like when it exploded into existence. It tasted so good my leg started shaking like when I, Ok nevermind that.

"This is amazing", I said. The gerbils were doing a virtual gymkhana in my head. Supercharged meth infused gerbils. This was not going to end well.

"Somehow I knew you would say that", Sydney said with a far off look. She snapped back to reality quickly.

"So you like it", she asked.

"I love it", I said. And I really did. It was flavored exactly how I liked it. Sugar, just a splash of cream and the perfect temperature. It was like she knew?

"Oracle Dreams, that's a unique name for a business", I observed.

"It was my gran's idea", Sydney says. "She was some kind of fortune teller back in the old days. She likes to kid me about living in a cave with other women and telling fortunes but I know she's just got to be joking."

"Oh, why is that", I asked and took another sip. It was like something< well something I couldn't write about here, had just drizzled liquid goodness on my tongue.

"Because silly, no one lives in caves anymore", she said. Her tone was gently mocking but not in a mean way. More like she thought I was being stupid on purpose to tease her. If only she knew I wasn't acting most days, sigh.

"Ah, of course", I said with a small laugh. "Though, my apartment kinda seems like one", I said half jokingly and half trying not to sound depressed. Maybe I could pay the cleaning staff from here to do my apartment? Maybe if I paid them they'd stop trying to kill me? Even the gerbils gave me the side eye on that thought.

"Well", Sydney said, "maybe I'll get to see it sometime." I choked and coffee shot out my nose.

"Huh, what", I tried to say while drowning. I was also trying to look around. I thought I heard some kind of hissing from near the bar. Grippy Socks Farms, here I come. I quickly looked back at Sydney, hoping she hadn't noticed.

"Oh not like that silly", she said with a smile. "You have a girlfriend and I don't poach other women's boyfriends. But maybe as friends? I just moved here and I don't really know anyone", she trailed off. She suddenly looked unsure of herself.

"Yeah, yeah of course. Absolutely", I said. "I don't have many either. Friends I mean so yeah, I'd really like that."

"Really? That's great", she replied. Her whole face lit up and she was all but dancing in place. "So, come by the shop sometime. I'll introduce you to Gran and we can talk coffee or maybe find something to do".

"That sounds really good", I said. I'd never had a girl want to be friends before. Hopefully it wouldn't bother Liz. She didn't seem like the jealous type, but how would I know? Sydney set down the other cups of coffee and muffins on the table.

"I've got to get back to the shop but I hope to see you soon", she said.

I'll definitely come by", I said.

"Great", she said before getting that faraway look again. "Dave, watch out for that mop". Then she turned and walked out without another word.

"Oh, okay", I said, not really knowing what she was talking about. I started to walk behind the bar as she gently closed the front door. And tripped over something. I fell straight on my face. I could have sworn I heard laughter somewhere in the bar. I looked up to figure out what I had tripped on and it was a mop handle. It had been wedged beneath the bar so I wouldn't see it. How had that gotten there? Wait, how had Sydney known?

Curious Things

I'M DONE. I HAVE HAD ENOUGH!!! Oh, hi, sorry about that. It's me again, Dave. Sorry, I think the intrusive thoughts just decided to exit at terminal velocity. That's embarrassing. It's been three whole days since I missed a kiss from Liz and now she's avoiding me. I even went by the temple and they all act like they've never heard of anyone named Liz. I don't know why they would pretend she doesn't exist but I'm getting really frustrated.

It wasn't my fault our kiss was interrupted. I wanted to kiss her. I really did. Just because I'm a caffeine addict and Sydney came in waving my one drug shouldn't be held against me. Liz had to understand it was a problem, an addiction really. Why did she run off anyway?

I did go to Sydney's shop to bathe my aching heart in delicious coffee. Which may have been a bad idea since I haven't slept in two days and I'm as jittery as a jonesing meth addict. It's weird because whenever I walk in I feel instantly better. Like the aura of the place is so inviting. But as soon as I leave, this mountain of crippling anxiety lands on me. And from someone who is the poster child for anxiety that's a lot. My childhood psychologist once told me there was a picture of me beside the diagnosis for anxiety in the DSM. Not sure whether he was joking or not. I mean, surely he was joking right?

And then, this morning, I come into the bar to open up and a mop bucket spills over my head. It had been rigged above the door to spill on whoever opened it. Damn Gurk or Gutrude or whoever. This was WAR! Even the gerbils were playing death metal and howling for blood. One of them had even donned a little red headband. They watch a lot of TV.

I had just managed to dry off and mop up the spill when the little bell above the door chimed. It was still an hour before opening but whatever. Maybe a customer would distract me from my rage and heart break.

A small man came in wearing an old brown tweed suit that was stylish but well worn. The suit jacket even had the old elbow pads and everything. Dude looked like a tweedy pimped out librarian. He looked sharp, but in a librarian kinda way. Small gold rimmed glasses perched on a small nose and his mousy brown hair blew gently in the wind as he tried to shut the door.

"I'm sorry sir", I said in my best customer service go away style voice. "We're not open yet. I must have just forgotten to lock the door."

"Oh, it's quite all right young man", the gentleman said. "I'm not a customer, I'm merely dropping off a package."

"Huh, I've never had anyone drop off a package before", I said.

"The owner of this, establishment, asked if I could deliver it personally", he said and looked around.

"Is he here", he asked hopefully.

"I'm sorry, but he never gets here before dark", I said. Apparently I had missed a wet spot and my underwear was soggy. The only thing worse than wet socks was wet underwear.

I was probably about to have high school flashbacks and I so wasn't ready for that.

"Well no matter", the tweedy man said. "My name is Matthias Mathers Marlow and I am the proprietor of Curious Things", he said. He stepped directly in front of me and produced a business card four inches from my nose. The card appeared so fast it snapped.

"Whoa dude", I said, "neat trick." Mr. Marlow smiled, clicked his heels and bowed slightly as I took his card. It read, "Curious Things, hard to find objects and curious baubles".

"So is this like an antique shop or something", I asked. I was so out of my depth. Mr. Marlow was so far away from our usual customers I really didn't know what to do. The gerbils were no help. They were sunk in fuzzy battle fury. Have you ever heard battle fury expressed in squeaks?

"Oh no young man", Mr Marlow stated. "I run a, well, a location service for different rare items. Those items with abilities or attributes much greater than the object itself."

"Oh, like what", I asked. I didn't know what he was talking about but I lived life one context clue at a time.

"Well, say you were a baker and had heard of a cake pan that could give your cakes the flavor of rainbows. Or a mythical coffee press that could make coffee taste so good it was as addictive as a street drug. But you had no idea how to locate such an object. That is when you would contact my fine establishment and, for a fee, I will procure the item for you."

"Things like that really exist", I asked in awe.

"Oh, young man, surely you jest", Mr. Marlow said while chuckling.

"What do you mean", I asked stupidly. Ok, look, I couldn't help it. There were no clues, none. Dude was talking like we were on a tv show. Things like that didn't really exist.

"Look around you yo... what is your name sir", Mr. Marlow asked abruptly. "I can't very well keep calling you young man,"

"Oh, uh, I'm Dave", I said.

"A pleasure to meet you, ahem, Dave", he said. "And yes, such things do exist. And many more just as extraordinary. Why the other day I delivered that coffee press...", he stopped abruptly. "Well, never mind that", he said.

"So you said you had a package for the owner", I asked. I didn't mean for it to sound so abrupt but I had the wet wedgie from hell and I could feel mop water trailing down the back of my leg.

"Oh, of course yo... I mean Dave. Here it is", he said, producing a small square box and handing it to me. "Goodness me, I'd lose my head if it wasn't attached."

"Ok, I'll just put it behind the bar", I said and turned that way.

"Can I offer you a drink for the trouble", I asked. Might as well be nice, poor guy was probably friends with the owner. What a horrible thought.

"Well, maybe just a quick nip", he said and sat down at the bar.

"Do you have brandy", he asked hopefully.

"Coming up", I said. I put the box in the safe under the bar and locked it. The walls seemed to shake a little and small motes of dust fell from the ceiling as I closed the safe. I started searching for the brandy on the shelves behind the bar. Brandy wasn't something that was requested a lot. After hunting for a minute I pulled out a bottle and blew the dust off the glass. It looked old but it was mid shelf so it couldn't be that expensive right?

I poured him a bit and set the bottle under the bar. Mr. Marlow took a gentle sip and sighed. He took his time and looked around the bar. It was an appraising glance. But I couldn't tell whether he was appraising the ambiance or the items in it. He spent a good bit of time silently examining the two old axes over the fireplace and goggled a little when he saw a portrait on the rear wall. Honestly it had always given me the creeps. I swear the people in it moved sometimes.

"So, to your question", Mr. Marlow said.

"I had a question", I asked. Yes, Dave smart, hehe.

"Yes things like what I describe do exist", he went on, obviously not listening to me. Which was probably good. More people should not listen to me really.

"I have been fortunate enough to locate magical hides that heal, rings that grant invisibility, a wolf pelt that grants virility if you take my meaning", I didn't but, "and recently an obelisk that can bring back the dead."

"Whoa, really", I asked. Nice old guy, completely crazy but nice, I thought to myself.

"You doubt me, do you Dave", he asked with a smile. Normally when people smile like that it means I'm in trouble. But crazy Mr. Marlow was harmless. Just look at how he was dressed.

"No, I didn't say that", I told him.

"It's quite all right Dave", he said. "A little proof never hurt anyone. You work in a, bar, filled with mysterious items."

"I do", I asked. I had never seen anything I'd consider mystical.

"So people pay you for weird objects", I asked.

"Curiosities Dave, things from different realities that cannot or should not exist. I have pulled the teeth of a naga for a client. For another I located the leg bone of a giant. A 'man of great renown' as one old book called it. I had one customer searching for a bed pan that shrieked when used. He is a horrible prankster really. The owner of this establishment likes items which can influence time and reality," he went on. "Why, last month, I located a locket that granted visions and a men's leather belt made from the hide of a minotaur. All of these things I find for my wonderful customers."

"That sounds really, um, amazing", I said.

"Ok", he said with a sigh. I think he could tell I wasn't buying it. "How about this", he asked and produced a small mirror from his pocket.

"Um, it's a mirror", I said. Dave, the newly crowned King of Observation, that's me. I could just hear the crowd cheering the coronation.

"It is in fact a mirror", Mr Marlow said. "But it will also show you the person you are most in love with. Such a wonderful thing really."

Thinking this was stupid I looked into the mirror. An older woman looked back at me. Grey hair, some wrinkles, but she obviously took care of herself. If I didn't know better it could almost be Liz's grandmother. Wait, this was a mirror, but there was a woman's face instead of mine shining in it. But it was a mirror. I flinched back a little and looked up to make sure Mr. Marlow's eyes weren't glowing. Nope, all normal. Mirrors don't show other peoples faces, do they? Had someone slipped me shrooms again? Why did I have a job which made me doubt my sanity this much? Or did I have the job because I doubted my sanity? Ow, ow, ow, I think I just got a mental nose bleed.

"I think your mirror's broke", I said while trying to stave off the incipient aneurysm from the thoughts currently pimp slapping my last three brain cells.

"Oh, how so", Mr Marlow asked concerned.

"The face in the mirror is of an old woman, not Liz's", I said. I didn't even know what to be confused by. A mirror that didn't mirror or a woman's face that wasn't Liz's. The gerbils were no help. They just kept squeaking "war" in gerbalesse.

"Perhaps, Dave, things are not as they seem with this Liz you speak of. Of all the things you must have seen, would that be so strange", he asked and finished his brandy before putting the mirror back in his pocket.

"Well, I must be off. Please give the owner my card and tell him I delivered the package", Mr. Marlow said and stood. "Oh, and do stop by the shop sometime. I have plenty of items for sell for a discerning young man such as you."

I stared at his retreating form as he marched sharply out the door. The little bell tinkled like the bell of a cage fight. It was all too confusing. The aneurysm abruptly averted for the moment, I refocused on something that wasn't confusing. Something that could warm the soul.

Round one to Gurk and the Gurkians but I would win the fight. This was WAR! How do you make booby traps anyway?

The Owner, The Priestess, and The Fool

So, hi, my name's Dave and I've spent the last couple of months telling everyone else's stories. Today I need to tell you about something that happened to me. I need to tell someone anyway. Today was one of those red letter days that can change a person. I'm writing this, telling all of you this, because I have to tell someone to save my sanity. Maybe to save myself, if I can even be saved.

It's only been three days since Mr. Marlow dropped off the mysterious package. Since then the bar has been full of some really rough, ahem, people. Everyone is walking around armed. Short George keeps coming in bristling with weapons. The lizard folk have been teaching people weird words and chants. I've seen everything from a fully armored knight to some kind of red skinned four foot tall, well being, who keeps coming in, going to the closet, and then leaving. The whole atmosphere is super tense right now. Even the gerbils are picking up on it and they never notice anything but coffee and snacks.

I went by Oracle Dreams for my usual coffee and muffin this morning and they were closed. There was some weird kind of notice on the door. It looked legal but was in a language I had never seen. Sans coffee and hungry I decided to come on into the bar early. It wasn't like I had anywhere else to go. I hadn't seen or heard from Liz in almost a week and Sydney was really my only other friend.

I opened the door slowly, looking for anything that could soak me or trip me. The bar was dark as I came in. It felt eerie. The shadows seemed to move and whisper to themselves. Or maybe that was just my mental state. I carefully walked around turning on the lights and shrugging out of my coat. As I came behind the bar there was a note pinned to the bar with one of those ninja daggers you see in the '70's Kung Fu Theater movies. I couldn't make out what the note said. Deciding to move tactically, i.e. not tripping on anything, I walked, or maybe hobbled, over to it. The word "beware" was scribbled across it.

"That's it, I can't take it anymore", I said to the empty bar. "My girlfriend dumped me, I haven't had coffee, and my crotch is still raw from the soaking! I'm not taking anymore", I screamed as I threw my coat on the ground.

"Gurk, do you hear me", I yelled. "I'm coming for you." My voice seemed to echo around the bar. Death metal was blaring in my head and the gerbils were armed up and ready to rock. Their screams for blood and vengeance were deafening, if squeaky. I started stomping around looking for implements of death and destruction before remembering the knife embedded in the note on the bar. That would do! Turning I went to grab it... And heard a door open at the back of the bar.

"Dave", the voice of the owner said, "could I see you back here for a minute?"

His voice caused me to stop so suddenly it probably looked like I was having a seizure. A resounding "eep" echoed through my head from the battle gerbils who were once again denied their battle song.

"Yes, sir", I said and gulped air. This couldn't be good. Oh, man, I was about to be fired wasn't I? I couldn't afford to be fired. How was I going to make rent? How could I afford coffee? Or worse, what if the owner sent me to an anger management class? Those were way worse! I walked towards the back of the bar and the owner motioned me inside.

"Come in Dave", he said, "sit down." The owner sat behind an old round bar table. Two steaming cups of coffee sat on the table in front of the chairs. Sitting next to the owner was a very large axe. A very large and shiny axe! The back room was dim as always but the single dim light seemed to gleam from the edge of the axe. Ok, so getting fired may not be so bad after all, I thought to myself.

"Um, sir, what's with the axe", I asked. I didn't intend to sit down if I might never get up again. Suddenly the battle gerbils were awful quiet. Traitors, the furry bunch of them.

"Oh, my apologies Dave", he said and chuckled a little nervously. "I had just finished cleaning it up. I apologize. That's really so unprofessional."

I nodded and went to sit down. The smell of the coffee had lured me in. Neither axe nor firing nor threat of death could stop my addiction. Was there a caffeine twelve step program? Coffee Anonymous?

"Sir, did this come from Oracle Dreams", I asked.

"Why yes it did. The owner and I have known each other for a long time. A very long time indeed", he said and chuckled. "Her granddaughter Sydney speaks very highly of you by the way."

"Yeah, we're friends", I said proudly. I had a friend. A girl friend, crap, I mean a friend who is also a girl. Oh I give up.

"She's a good girl Dave, maybe you should ask her out", the manager said. I looked at him stupidly. I didn't know what to say to that. Sydney was certainly an amazing person and great to be around. And she was adorable with her cheerfulness and anime girl energy, but we were just friends, right?

"Oh well, that's not really my place as your employer. Just friendly advice is all", he said with a sigh. "Oh, I almost forgot, do you know my name Dave?"

"Your name, sir", I asked. "It isn't 'the owner'?"

"No, Dave", he said sighing. He sighed a lot around me really. "It's Vyern."

"Vern", I asked.

"No, Vyern", he said a little angrily.

"Born", I asked. I just couldn't seem to pronounce it like he did.

"No, say it with me Dave. Vee-yorn with a hard orn sound", he said pedantically. I almost giggled but managed to contain it. Hard orn, oh that was too much for my twelve year old self to handle.

"Do you know why you're here Dave", he asked and sighed for a third time. See, I told you. His whole demeanor changed with the question. It was all business suddenly.

"Um, to set up the bar", I asked.

"Not exactly", he said and chuckled again. "Today is your ninety day performance review", he said. He opened a green file folder and pulled out a few sheets of paper. "Now..."

Before he could continue there was a massive crash from the front of the bar. I could hear footsteps racing through the bar. The manager shot up, yanking his axe to him and flinging the table to the back of the room. He stood facing the door. Had he suddenly gotten bigger? Muscles rippled in his arms as he gripped the axe. His red hair and beard seemed to move in a wind that was definitely not blowing in this dingy little room.

The door to the back room flew open and Liz filled the doorway. She was so beautiful. Her chestnut hair blew in the wind and her robes clung to her body. I couldn't help but notice that her chest was heaving. Her hands were engulfed in a bright golden energy. It shimmered like light through the fin of a goldfish. Which was ironic really. Her eyes seemed to glow with the same golden light.

"You shall not sacrifice him", Liz bellowed.

"Elizabeth", he said, "what are you doing here? I told you to never come back."

"I will not let you sacrifice this poor dolt for your war", she said. I stood up. Sacrifice, dolt, what was she saying? I had just started to be happy to see her. Now I was even more confused than when I was talking to the owner. I mean Vyern.

"No one's going to sacrifice Dave", he said and lowered his axe. "Dave is a vital member of my staff. I've grown Elizabeth, unlike you", he said and gestured towards the poor shattered doors.

"You're not going to sacrifice him", she asked confused.

"No, I'm not", he said. "Wait, why do you care what happens to Dave? He doesn't follow your oh so wonderful goldfish."

"Well, um", Liz was suddenly looking anywhere but at us. The golden light had faded from around her and she seemed to shrink a little.

"Oh, Elizabeth, I knew you liked them young but this is ridiculous", Vyern said and shook his head.

"You don't get to tell me what to do", she hissed at him. "You gave up that right, remember?"

"You left me, I didn't give up anything", Vyern raged right back.

"Whoa, wait just a minute", I said loudly. Both of them stopped and looked at me. And suddenly I was an inch from death again. Yay, solid ground!

"Were you two a thing", I asked.

"Yes Dave, apparently my ex-wife has the hots for you", Vyern said and spat on the floor.

"Wife, we were never married, you clod", she said.

"I distinctly remember getting married Elizabeth", he shot back.

"Ha", she said. "You never even sacrificed the virgins. You just lied to the Old Ones because you were too lazy."

"So, um, you knew about that huh", Vyern asked sheepishly. "You looked so beautiful that day. You lit up that whole reality and I was so proud. Was I really supposed to wait three days for the sacrifice? What about our honeymoon?"

A pause ensued. The gerbils were hiding under their beds and I was trying to catch up. Sacrifice, dolt, ex-wife, sacrifice again? Could someone stop this ride, I wanted to get off.

"Of course I knew about that. And what about our honeymoon?", she said. "And yes I'm interested in Dave. How could I not be? He's honest and sweet, unlike you", she said.

"He tries so hard to be good. I miss what that's like", she said softly. Vyern untensed or uncoiled or whatever.

"Are you trying to say you love my bartender", he asked.

"Well love, maybe not love, yet", she hedged.

"And does he know, you know", he trailed off.

"Do I know what", I asked in the silence. A very pregnant silence. Wait, pregnant? We hadn't even kissed yet.

"Dave, there's something I have to tell you", she said and reached a hand towards me.

"I'll say", Vyern said.

"Shut up", she spat back at him before continuing. "Dave, I don't always look like this", she said.

"Oh, you mean make up or something", I asked stupidly. Vyern snorted and she shot him a nasty look.

"Dave, I'm sorry but I lied to you. I'm not a simple priestess. I am the Head Priestess of the Church of the Holy Goldfish and I have been for a long time."

"Like how long", I asked. Hey, I couldn't think of anything else ok?

"About ten thousand human years", Vyern piped in.

As he said this, Liz began to age before my eyes. Her chestnut hair turned gray and wrinkles set into her face. Her body shifted a little under her robes. She didn't look, like, ancient or anything. Maybe a youthful sixty with a really good skin care regimen.

"Liz", I croaked in shock.

"I'm sorry Dave", she stammered. "I didn't think you would like me unless I was young and pretty again".

"But...But...", was all I could say. She was still beautiful. Still amazing, but she had lied to me.

"I'll just step out and let you two discuss this amongst yourselves", Vyern said. Before he could move we heard a voice from what used to be the front door of the bar.

"Hello", a cultured male voice called. "I'm Chadwick Bartholomew from the Demonic Business Bureau? Anyone here", he called.

Vyern and Liz looked at each other for a second before they both said, "Stay here". They looked at each other again.

"You finally choosing a side", he asked her.

"Yes, but only to protect Dave", she said softly.

"That'll have to do", he said and hefted his axe before walking out the door. Liz followed him but stopped in the doorway to look back at me.

"I'm sorry Dave", she said. "But I do love you". She turned and walked into the bar behind Vyern. I was definitely not just waiting back here. I yelled at the gerbils to cowboy up and walked out behind them. It was brave, if you spell brave as s-t-u-p-i-d.

The front of the bar was in shambles. Standing just inside was a man of average height with an average haircut, average gray suit, and an average face. The kind of guy who could talk to you for ten minutes and you'd barely remember him.

"Chadwick", Vyern asked mockingly.

"You can call me Chad", he said brightly. "I'm here today to serve you this." He reached into his suit and pulled out a yellow slip of paper. It was the same color as the one on the door to Oracle Dreams this morning.

"And just what is this", Vyern asked.

"This", and Chad waved the paper. "This is a Cease and Desist to stop all business at this location. Your business is being closed by the DBB for neighborhood improvement and gentrification."

"And does this paper close my temple as well", Liz asked.

"No, your temple is exempt under the Community Religious Support Act", Chad said brightly.

"The hell it is", Vyern yelled and took up a battle stance. Liz's hands began to glow again and she motioned me to hide behind the bar. Suddenly a whole group of green skinned goblin like things ran out of every corner of the bar waving axes and knives. The leader of the green skinned goblins was blowing a small horn that was tremendously loud. It was the kind of sound that summoned genetic memories of running with wolves and breaching castle gates.

The sky began to tremble and I heard a sound like I had only heard once before. Oh, no, not again. Giant tentacles fell from the sky and a sound akin to madness howled through the wind. Through the window I could see people swarming to the front of the bar. Short George and his friends rode up on giant hounds brandishing swords. The lizard folk were hovering in the air whispering sounds I couldn't understand. I could hear horses hooves and could only assume the knight was out there as well. From around the corner of the building Sydney ducked inside, an older woman being towed behind her. Sydney ducked behind the bar where I was cowering in fear and confusion.

"Are you ok", she yelled over the maelstrom.

"We're all going to die", I yelled back. I don't think she heard me. She just grinned and held up her thumb. How could she think any of this was good?

"You may kill us, but you will never take our businesses", Vyern yelled and coiled to spring at Chad.

"Tut tut", Chad said. "None of this is necessary, you know. If you had objections all you had to do was fill out form 50361 in triplicate and submit them." The howling stopped and everyone froze for a minute. Even the screams of madness suddenly stilled.

"Huh", Vyern said while still brandishing his axe. I wasn't the only one who used "huh" as a noun and a verb! I wasn't the only one. I felt like doing a happy dance as the gerbils gave me side eye.

"Yes, of course, all you had to do was attend a meeting and fill out the forms. We would have even helped you to do so. All of this is entirely unnecessary, you know."

"You didn't even talk to them", Liz yelled at Vyern and swatted him on the bicep. She obviously regretted this as she stood shaking her hand.

"Well, um, you see", Vyern started.

"If you object this strongly perhaps we can discuss the issue", Chad said. "Perhaps over a brandy?" Muttering broke out from everyone outside and the sky shook as Daniel's dad returned to wherever he came from. Everyone started to break up.

"Wait, all we have to do is fill out some stupid forms and you'll stop trying to close us", Vyern asked.

"In triplicate, but yes. I'd even go so far as to let you list all the businesses that wish exemption to be listed on one form", he said.

"We only wish to help", he said with a razor toothed smile. Guy could give a Great White an inferiority complex. Cursing could be heard from outside as the crowd broke up. Vyern looked sheepishly at Liz who hissed in disgust.

"Hey, we all make mistakes", Vyern said, trying to appease everyone. Liz shook her head and came over to the bar.

"Dave, when you've had time to process all this, please come see me at the temple. Please, just give me a chance". She stopped, gave Sydney a dark look, and then exited the bar.

"Your girlfriend is really intense", Sydney said. "Come on Gran, let's go find this form and get opened back up", she stated cheerfully as she and the older lady walked out.

"Dave, how about a bottle and two glasses", Vyern asked. "If there are any left", he said observing the carnage. I dug under the bar and found the bottle of Brandy from the other day and two glasses as Vyern and Chad sat at the only intact table in the bar to talk business.

One of the small goblin figures came up and hugged me around the upper thigh. Her face was a little too close to my groin for comfort but I let it ride. Was this Gurk's sister? Geez, what if it was Gurk?

"You all right for a stupid human", the goblin figure with the horn said. "I will let you date sister", he said before walking off into the closet. His sister followed blowing me kisses over her shoulder. Oh, yea gods, really?

I took the bottle and glasses to the table and was thoroughly ignored by Vyern and Chad. It sounded like they were talking tax code or something. I looked around at the damage. The front half of the bar was destroyed.

"Dave", I heard Vyern call my name. "Take the day off. You've earned it", he said.

I sighed in relief and turned to grab my coat from behind the bar. Before I could reach it I heard a whisper in my ear.

"And stay away from the Temple", it said. It was Vyern's voice. I turned to look back at him. His eyes glowed as he looked at me. They glowed.

Aftermath

Hi guys it's me again, Dave. Yeah you probably knew that already, I know. I'm sorry I just couldn't sleep. It's only been a few hours since I found out everything about Liz. Her history with the owner, the fact that she had been lying to me, all of it. I know Vyern said take the day off but I really wish he hadn't. I really need to be doing something right now.

I made my way home after the whole fiasco at the bar. I must have stopped a few times on the walk home since it was dark by the time I got here. I was kind of in a haze. To be honest, I still am. I mean, it's a lot to process. Did Liz really lie? Sure she faked her age, but who doesn't really? Or was I just being a sap? I didn't really know anything about her except that she was nice to me. Wasn't that enough? Was it enough?

I puttered around in my dingy little apartment for a while, just trying to mull things over. I was about to do something really desperate like wash the dishes when there was a knock at the door. I considered not answering it when the knocking became a pounding. I walked over and jerked the door open. And had to look down.

Four Gurkians stood in the doorway carrying, or dragging really, a man in a flowing golden robe. Since they were all between three and four feet tall the guy in the robe probably had some serious rug rash. They looked at me, blinking, until their leader spoke up.

"Move, stupid human", he said. I jumped out of the way and they drug the figure inside.

"Gurk, what the hell", I demanded.

"Gurk not like you, but Gurk not want you dating sister. Gurk thought you could question man about priestess", Gurk said. I quickly shut the door behind them. One of them drug a wobbling kitchen chair into the middle of the floor and they threw the poor guy up on it. I could clearly see a knot on his head where they must have hit him.

"And how am I supposed to do that", I asked Gurk.

"Stupid human cuts off mans toes till he talks", Gurk said. "Stupid human must have knife?"

"My name is Dave", I told him.

"Stupid human fits better", Gurk said and the others laughed. Great, just great. The man in the robe moaned, coming around from the land of the unconscious. The gerbils were as stunned as I was, all I heard were confused sounds in my head. Some help they were.

"Gurk, I can't torture someone to find out about Liz", I explained

"Fine, Gurk do for stupid human as friendship", he said with a burbling sigh.

"No", I said, "I mean that torture is wrong." Gurk sighed again.

"Hey, what am I doing here", the robe guy mumbled, coming around.

"You fell", I said quickly, "and my friends brought you here."

"Ouch", the guy screamed as Gurk poked him in the shin with a wicked looking knife.

"Gurk stop that", I said.

"Gurk", the man asked, "Gurk the Destroyer?" The guy was suddenly terrified and managed to focus on the small violent individual in front of him.

"I am Gurk", Gurk said with dignity. A wet spot immediately formed on the guy's robes. Great, didn't I mop up enough urine at work? Now it was going to be in my carpet.

"Oh Goldfish, please don't kill me", the guy said and started to sob.

"Noone's going to kill anyone", I said.

"Gurk kill if no answer questions", Gurk contradicted but turned and winked at me. I think he was having fun.

"What do you want to know", the guy asked, blubbering.

"Tell stupid human about High Priestess", Gurk instructed.

"Elizabeth, the High Priestess", the guy asked. "She's been head of the temple for eons. No one knows anything about her."

"You sure you not know", Gurk asked, flourishing his knife.

"I swear", the guy said and started out right crying. He was terrified. Terrified by Gurk for some strange reason.

"Ok, you go", Gurk said with a shrug.

"What", the guy asked.

"What", I echoed.

"He no know nothing", Gurk said, "we kidnap another one."

"Wait Gurk", I said, "you don't need to kidnap anyone else." Gurk sighed again.

"Gurk tried for you, you no date sister", Gurk insisted.

"I promise I won't date your sister", I told him.

"Sister kill me if she knew I didn't want date", he said. He was very serious about that.

"I give you my word", I said. Gurk stared at me for a minute and then nodded.

"You go", Gurk said to the guy. The dude moved fast for a man with a probable concussion. He was out the door in a flash.

"You have mess, must clean", Gurk said with a laugh, leaving with his cohorts, and leaving me with a mess on the carpet. At least, one more stain wouldn't be noticed. I stood there for a few minutes and then closed the door. I was contemplating just leaving the clean up for another time when there was another knock at the door. I jerked the door back open, looking for anything to keep me from having to clean up one more puddle of piss.

"Gurk, enough is enough", I said as I flung open the door. I stopped speaking and hit a fugue state when I saw who was standing in the hall.

"Dave", Liz said, "can we talk?"

I Met a Vampire

Hi, it's me, Dave, with another thrilling adventure from the Hellhound Bar. I'm sure everyone has plenty of questions about what happened when Liz knocked on my door, but that's kind of private. I know, I know, but some things a man needs to keep to himself. We've decided to try and work everything out. I don't know if it'll work but I'm willing to give it a shot. Sydney is dubious about it, but I'm willing to try. Dubious, he he, what a great word. That thesaurus Mr. Marlow gave me is really helping!

Today is the grand reopening of the bar and I'm not sure whether to be excited or to be filled with mortal dread really. It's only been a week since the place was demolished but Vyern says the DBB has been a big help in the reconstruction. From the look of the place I believed him.

I was just cutting limes to stock the bar when I heard the bell above the door give a happy little tinkle. I looked up to see a woman entering the bar wearing blue scrubs. You know, like the ones they wear on TV. She had chestnut hair and a beautiful face. Well, it would be beautiful if she wasn't scowling so hard. Poor lady had resting bitch face so bad she could scare most Karens right out of their official haircut.

"Welcome to the Hellhound Bar", I said cheerfully, "what can I get you."

"Why the hell are you so chipper", the lady asked as she sat on the barstool in front of me.

"Just trying to be helpful", I said, cringing inside. Just great, our first customer on reopening would have to be the difficult type. Karens, man.

"Vyern said you'd have what I'm drinking", she said.

"You know Vyern", I asked. A small chill ran down my spine. Friends of the owner could be really dangerous. I wasn't sure I was ready for that.

"He said to tell you it was in the cooler at the end of the bar in a green bottle", she told me. She had completely glossed over my question which seemed odd but I didn't care. I walked down to the end of the bar and opened the little refrigerator. Sure enough, there were four green bottles filled with a thick liquid. I pulled one out.

"What is this stuff", I asked.

"Don't worry about it, just pour", she said.

"Coming right up", I said in my best king of customer service voice. I pulled down a stemmed glass and filled it half full. The stuff was thick and dark red. Kinda smelled metallic to be honest. The gerbils were clamoring in my head, screaming that there was danger but I didn't see it. The lady picked up the glass and took a long sip. Her whole face relaxed and a smile bloomed there. Her shoulders relaxed and she sat up straighter. She almost seemed to have transformed.

"I'm so sorry for my attitude", she said with a winsome smile. "Mornings are so dreadful for me Dave."

"Um, how did you know my name", I asked. Panic filled me for a moment.

"Why, your nametag, of course", she said. Right, I kept forgetting I had to wear the damned thing now.

"Oh, right, duh", I said. "Can I get you anything else?"

"A little company would be nice", she said.

"Well, I can hang around for a bit if you like", I told her, "the only other person who might be here is Mickey and you really don't want to be around him."

"You'll do just fine Dave", she purred. I gulped, Oh man, oh man, things were just panning out with me and Liz, I didn't need a woman flirting with me!

"So, um, what brings you here", I asked.

"My job", she said while playing with the stem of her glass.

"What do you do", I asked. See, I could make small talk.

"I'm a phlebotomist", she said. "Which is a damned strange job for a vampire if you think about it."

"You're a what", I asked in shock.

"A phlebotomist dear", she asid.

"No, I mean...", I trailed off.

"Oh, a vampire you mean", she asked.

"Yeah", I said and gulped again. The gerbils were shrieking in furry terror and I was paralyzed.

"You don't discriminate, do you Dave", she asked while leaning over the bar towards me. I could just see the hint of fang peeking from her upper lip.

"We do have the right to refuse service to anyone who tries to eat the bartender", I said. She laughed so hard I thought she was going to spill her drink.

"Oh man, is that blood", I said, realizing what I had served her.

"Yes indeed", she said, "and a rather good vintage too."

"Ok, so like, am I in danger", I asked. Ok so maybe it squeaked a little when I said it, so what.

"As dinner, no", she said, "but for other things perhaps."

"I'm, I'm, I'm", I stammered before seizing on something else. "But it's daylight out."

"Yes it is, Dave, you're cute when you're observant", she said with a smile. "The sun here at Center is different. We can be out in the day or night here."

"Good to know", I said. The gerbils had been right. But was I in danger of dying or was my virtue in more danger than my life?

"So how did you get into phlebotomy", I asked, trying to distract her.

"Being a vampire isn't as glamorous as it used to be", she said. "Some of us had to get day jobs to survive. It's not all virgins and castles anymore."

"Do you like it", I asked.

"I like the job", she said. "The administration is rather demonic. And sometimes it's hard to keep focus drawing blood. The temptation of just a sip is rather challenging." She gave me a full fang grin as she said it.

"Sounds difficult", I said. The fangs were wigging me out a little. I mean I didn't care what anyone was, I wasn't speciest. But I didn't want to be a human juice box either.

"Have you ever been tempted, Dave", she asked in a sultry voice, "it can be a very powerful thing." She reached across the bar and stroked my hand which had been polishing the wooden surface until a minute ago. I could feel a jolt of something, attraction or magnetism, with her touch. I must have been blushing all the way to my hairline because she laughed and let go.

"I only have a few minutes before my shift, but I wanted to meet the cute bartender Vyern spoke so highly of", she said and hopped off the barstool. "I'll stop back by for another drink soon Dave."

"Ok, well, thanks", I said, not knowing what else to say or who had run me over with a truck full of stupid. All I knew was that all my blood wasn't in my brain any longer. No, it was significantly lower in my body.

"Oh and Dave", the woman called, standing at the door.

"Yeah", I squeeked.

"My name's Mona", she said with a wink before walking out. Oh by the Sacred goldfish, what had Vyern gotten me into now?

I Met A Blob's Chauffeur

Hi again everybody it's me, Dave I mean. I know you probably get tired of me constantly opening stories like that but it's just kind of how I think. I'm not slow or anything, I just think differently. My mom always said I was special.

So it's been a day or two since the lovely Mona showed up at the bar and the questions are swirling in my head hard enough to drown the gerbils. Did Vyern send her here? Or was she actually interested in me? Does it really matter since things are kinda working out with Liz?

I've been kind of stumbling around in the bar trying to find everything since the destruction. Gurk and I are sort of getting along, kind of. It's becoming a weird relationship between he and I. On the one hand I think he wants to stab me and on the other hand I think he actually likes me deep down. Really really deep down.

Liz has been absent for the last day or so. She's been doing some weird ritual at the Temple of the Goldfish. I stopped by Oracle Dreams this morning and got an amazing muffin. Sydneys been very supportive but she thinks I really need to leave Liz alone and I'm just not ready to do that yet.

I managed to get to the bar today about 13 minutes late but Vyern wasn't there so, if you don't tell, I won't. I hurried to open the door and to turn on all the lights. Vyern said he'd get us a new jukebox soon but I've never seen a jukebox in here and I'm afraid of what people like our customers would do to it. I could just see Short George whacking it with an axe.

I hadn't even gotten to bring in ice or restock the coolers when the little bell over the door rang. I really hate that bell. Every time it rings it signals the possibility of my impending doom and I don't need a harbinger to tell me that I'm about to die. I already know that.

I turned to see a man come in wearing a black suit and a black derby cap. He looked straight out of some weird seventies TV show. He had blonde hair under the hat and a blonde goatee. He was maybe six five or six six and looked like an Ichabod Crane reject. I definitely did not have a good feeling about this.

"Good afternoon, my name is Christos", the man said.

"Hi Christos, my name is Dave. What can I do for you", I asked my best customer service voice.

"A beer would be wonderful," the man said and sat down at the bar with a sigh.

"Any particular brand that you would like," I asked and gave him a smile. Maybe he'd even tip.

"Oh anything that you have on tap," Christos said.

"Well we just got this one in stock," I said and began pouring him a nice dark ale.

"Yes that looks like it'll do" he said, "of course to be honest anything will do at this point."

"So what do you do for a living," I asked as I passed him the ale.

"I am the chauffeur for a very exclusive client", the man said, "and honestly he's a real pain in the butt."

"Oh I've had clients like that", I said, "it's never a good day, is it?"

"No it is not, it is actually quite difficult", he said and slammed a hand against the bar in frustration.

"I'm sorry I know what that feels like, if there's anything else I can do", I said, and began trying to stock the bar without him noticing. No one needed to know I'd been late.

"Perhaps you can help me", Christos said.

"And how would I do that", I asked, beginning to get nervous. It was never good when anybody took me up on something I said. They should know I wasn't thinking when I spoke.

"How does one land a job such as this", he asked and made an expansive gesture around the bar.

"You want to be a bartender", I asked.

"I am certainly considering a change in employment", he said.

"How long have you been, well, a chauffeur", I asked.

"For around a hundred years", he said.

"A hundred years? What the, I mean, have vehicles been around that long", I asked him.

"Yes, Dave, vehicles have been around that long. If not the motor driven kind then also the horse and carriage", he said.

"What would bring a person into that kind of work", I asked.

"I always like to be on the go. Seemed like a good career for a man without prospects to constantly see new places", the man explained to me.

"Yeah I guess it could at that", I said.

"But this new client, he's just a little bit more than I can handle", he said.

"What about this client is so awful, if you don't mind my asking", I said. The gerbils were going nuts. They were holding up giant signs reading danger ahead. But was I smart enough to listen, obviously not.

"Well, for one thing", Christos said, "he's a blob."

"Hey", I said, "it's not nice to make fun of peoples weight."

"No Dave", Christos said and sipped his ale, "he's literally a blob. A gelatinous mass."

"What, like really", I demanded.

"Really Dave", he said. "Do you have any idea how challenging that is?"

"Um, no", I said, "probably not."

"This is my fourth suit he's slimed this week", Christos said with a great deal of heat. "He eats everything! Yesterday I had to pull over and hold his door while he enveloped a rotten piece of roadkill. The smell was horrendous."

"Oh, dude, that's gross", I said.

"Have you ever tried to clean roadkill sludge out of carpet", he asked.

"No but I once met a guy with a tentacle porn 'stache", I said helpfully.

"Really", he asked, "how strange."

"And at least once a week someone tries to kill me", I went on. "Oh, and I could tell you stories about all the urine I've had to mop up."

"Well, that takes the glamor out of being a bartender doesn't it", he said and drained his beer.

"Dude, it's a rough gig", I told him.

"Well, I guess I should get back", he said. "My client has a date."

"How does that work", I asked.

"I do not know", he said, "but I dearly hope never to see two blobs have intimate relations." He shuddered and stood up from the bar. He dropped a twenty on the bar and turned to leave. He was halfway to the door when he turned back to me.

"I guess my job isn't as bad as I thought", he said and took one last look around before walking out. That was a horrible thought. If seeing blobs boink was better than my job, I needed to reevaluate my life. Yeah, I probably needed to take a long hard look at my career path... NAH!

Curious Introductions

My name is Matthias Mathers Marlow and I am the proprietor of Curious Things. Recently a young man named Dave told me of his plights and how he sent his thoughts into the universe on this internet device thingy. Dave is a curious young man and has no idea what he really is, and I've learned to pay attention to the actions of such people. They are frequently well ahead of the rest of the multiverse in how the future shapes itself. So, I thought, maybe I should do so as well. If nothing else, this may very well serve as a chronicle for the next proprietor of my wonderful shop.

No one knows when or how Curious Things was established. Or established itself really. But every once in a while a new proprietor will be chosen and the old one... well, never mind that. Suffice it to say it is a wonderful shop filled with the bizarre and unusual from across the multiverse. I myself was a newly minted archaeologist when I stumbled into the shop. It's wares enthralled me with such history. I fell in love so deeply I could not leave. Perhaps it is like that for all of us. Who can say?

So for now, allow me to impart the tale of my most recent acquisition. A few days ago I departed our wonderful dimension in search of the Mirror of Urlrich. In a universe not far from my own there once was a mighty warrior. Isn't there always? Just once could history not have a mighty lover instead? Or perhaps a mighty scholar? No, we are gentle or wise in the annals of history. But I digress. Urlrich was a great warrior of Vyern's people, though a few generations removed. The legends state that he was in possession of a hand mirror which he carried into every battle. It is said that this mirror would whisper to him every grooming day. Supposedly it showed Urlrich his path for each new conquest.

Vyern and Urlrich's people are strange, really. They had the remarkable custom of taking one day a week and doing nothing but grooming themselves. Their beautification rituals were intense, especially the men. Why go to such lengths just to be covered in the blood of your enemies the next day, I ask you? Wouldn't one wish to groom themselves after the battle? Or perhaps they did and we just do not know? There is so much we do not know to this day. Fascinating, really.

At any rate I knew I would not find the mirror in Vyern's universe. The ancient oral legend on Vyern's world describes Urlrich walking into a great whirlwind instead of dying. The legend describes Mighty Urlrich, ugh this again, surrounded by the bodies of his enemies and his slain comrades, the last warrior standing after a horrible battle. Bereft and exhausted he felt he could not face another sunrise and so he had determined he would die standing, surrounded by his kith and kin. But as he raised his sword to end his life, a great wind came upon him and a whirlwind surrounded his body, taking him physically to the lands of the dead. Alas, there is no mention of ruby slippers, however incongruous.

And honestly, the legend would stop there. If not for my brilliant friend Truna. She has been my companion through many adventures and is an amazing metalsmith of all mediums.

From fine jewelry to amazing weapons she can make metal sing to her as she shapes it. But what many do not know is that she possesses a beautiful mind and wit as well. She tells me she has discovered a written legend from the time of Urlrich that tells his story after the whirlwind. If this is true, the mirror may very well exist.

Leaving Curious Things I traveled quickly in the early morning towards The Depot. The Depot is managed by The Entities of Entropy, which has recently become not only a race but a business conglomerate in the interdimensional travel industry. A curious race, neither here nor there really. Sorry, I couldn't resist the joke.

Truna had somehow carved out her own pocket dimension long ago and getting to her was difficult to say the least. Handing my blood token to the conductor I had to queue for a near eternity before I was allowed to move through the gates and through space and time to her home dimensional portal. Bureaucracy is always the stronghold of the simple minded. Where has the spark of life gone from the species of the multiverse anyway? Oh right, that Nyarlathotep chappy wasn't it? Never mind...

Truna's pocket dimension was all forest with a quaint cottage and a huge barn behind it where she worked. I still have not puzzled out why the foliage on the trees happens to be purple and the sky black, but if it makes her happy, who am I to judge? I could hear the hammer blows coming from the barn and stopped to watch the gray smoke climb from the chimney into the night sky. It was a peaceful sight in the search for the legend of such a war-like person. I moved around the plant-covered front of the cottage and towards the barn.

Truna had a real talent for plants and they were everywhere around and throughout her cottage abode. Of course, I could not recall anything Truna did not have a talent for. So maybe I was slightly envious, but one should be when confronted with such ability.

I approached the barn rather cautiously. I did not wish to startle Truna as the last time I had done so, she had buried an axe in the post next to my head. I still hear it quivering in the wood in my nightmares. Alas, that was not what I was dreading. I was more worried about... Oh bother...

From behind the barn I heard a horrific howling. The kind that froze the soul in dread. The sound pitched higher and I felt that existential fear of the hunted. The soul shrinking feeling of one doomed and soon to be devoured. I froze, knowing what was next. I had forgotten... too late I realized I had forgotten the puppy treats...

From the shrubs behind me a six foot hound leapt from the perpetual night and landed all three hundred pounds directly on my chest. I stumbled back and was tripped by a second furry body. It had apparently snuck behind me and laid at my feet so the first fur missile could trip me easier. I lay crushed under the fangs and fur of a snarling cross between a wolf, a malinois, and a demon from hell with its teeth an inch from my nose and drool dripping down my neck and into the collar of my linen shirt. I realized too late that the hounds had laid an ambush for me. Oh, what devious, brutish, hellish beasts they were!

"Pinky, Sam, get over here", a warm contralto voice bellowed from the doorway of the barn. Or, I assumed it was the doorway rather, as I was pinned and being marinated in drool. What was Truna feeding these monsters to give them breath this bad? Was there a sewage leak somewhere? I mean, really?

"Pinky, get off me", I wheezed as my ribs began to collapse. It wasn't going to eat me, it was going to crush me first. The hound stopped growling as Sam moved up beside him. After a considering stare Pinky rolled out a huge black tongue and licked the entire side of my head. Not my face, my entire head. Sam woofed softly in what could only be humor. They always did this to me.

"Truna", I yelped as Pinky went for a second lick. I was afraid I wouldn't have a face left if Pinky managed a third. His tongue was as rough as sandpaper and the stench from his breath was quickly causing all the oxygen in the area to flee for its safety.

"You forgot the puppy treats again, didn't you", Truna asked as she grabbed Pinky by the scruff of his neck and hauled him off of me. The muscles in her arms corded as she pulled the mountainous mutt from my body like he was weightless. Sam sat patiently, her tongue lolling from between teeth that would give a werewolf an inferiority complex and panting slightly.

"I don't want to talk about it", I wheezed and held up my hand for Truna to help me up. She grasped my hand firmly but was surprisingly gentle as she brought me back to my feet. Truna was a conundrum of beauty, brawn, and one of the most amazing minds I had ever met. I daresay I might have had a slight school boy crush on her. But alas, I could never infringe on our friendship enough to dare. Perhaps this is why there are no mighty archeologists?

"You know they wait for you right", Truna said with a laugh.

"Lie in wait is more accurate", I said huffily as I dusted off my suit. I mean really, this was a bespoke item!

"Why do you let them do it", she asked and looked at me.

"Do what", I asked. I may not have been paying attention. Truna was wearing very little and I hadn't noticed until I was bent over dusting off my shoes. Standing back up was a glorious indulgence of the female form as every inch of her, barring a few straps of leather, was present in my gaze.

"Come off it", she said. "You're just as good in a bar room brawl as I am and almost as strong, why do you let them take you down?"

"I don't let them", I exclaimed belligerently. "They are hellhounds. They are cunning and forceful brutes with unnatural abilities. How could I stand up to them", I demanded.

"Whatever", she said and turned back to the barn. As soon as she started walking away both hounds jumped up on my chest and I petted them ferociously. Ok, so maybe I liked them. So what?

We all followed Truna into the barn. It was a magnificent sight to behold. Tables and racks lined every wall and it was an odd mixture of the most ancient blacksmithing and jeweling tools mixed with the latest scientific equipment. Side by side with that were toolboxes of every shape and size. It was a tinker's shop of wonders for the barbarically inclined.

"I love what you've done with the place", I said and looked for a clean place to sit. I doubted I would find one.

"One more remark from you and I won't tell you what I found", Truna said without looking at me. She was intent on something rather intricate on the workbench.

"Oh, heavens", I said. "I tremble in fear.

"Sit", she said and snorted at me. I found a rather worn work stool that looked reasonably free from dust and oil and settled regally upon it. No way would I give Truna the satisfaction of thinking I had obeyed like Pinky and Sam. I sat quietly knowing this would irritate her. It was a game we both enjoyed. The mock battles of siblings or lovers... no wait... nevermind.

"Alright so... Happy Birthday", she said and threw the object at me. I caught it as it flew through the air. Looking at my stinging palm, Truna had a serious fast ball, I saw an old fashioned pocket watch. It was silver and the cover had a small book lying open engraved upon it. Opening it I could see the clock face and, through it, all the intricate gears that kept the watch working.

"This is beautiful", I said.

"You're welcome you old geezer", she said with a smile.

"How old are you pretending to be now", she asked.

"A ginger thirty nine thank you very much", I stated.

"More like one hundred and thirty nine", she mumbled but I ignored her.

"Thank you", I said again.

"You're very welcome", she said and smiled. She got this far off look in her eyes for a moment then suddenly blushed furiously and looked away. "Anyway, the mirror", she said.

"Yes please, the mirror", I said. We were both deflecting and we knew it.

"Your man Urlrich was teleported to sub dimension 503614-B", Truna started.

"Stop, you know I don't keep up with these tiresome bureaucratic and idiotic designations", I said.

"Fine, fine", she said. "He was transported to the glass dimension by a wandering being who thought it would be funny."

"You mean that weird mirror dimension", I asked. In the dimension I was asking about, everything was made of a reflective surface, mostly glass but there were rocks that were highly reflective as well as almost every other surface.

"That's the one", she said. "As you can imagine he was almost immediately struck blind and half the skin was scorched from his body. One can only assume serious genetic damage as well but we'll never know. From there he found his way to Center".

"Center", I gasped. "You mean our dimension"?

"Your dimension", she countered. "Don't lump me in with you madmen living in an intelligent microcosm".

"My apologies", I said and executed a mock bow to her.

"Apparently he was taken in by some of the underdwellers there", she continued.

"And...", I prompted.

"And", she said with a smile, "it's still there".

"You're joking", I said.

"Nope", she was grinning broadly now. "But, it's in the Underland".

It was at this point that I may have muttered a few words unsafe for publication which should never be used in polite company.

"Exactly", Truna said. "So, do you think you'll need help"?

"From who", I asked. I was genuinely puzzled.

"From me you overdressed popinjay", she said.

"Didn't you start a war with Rothna over a bet and wipe out half his tribe with a fork the last time you were in the Underland", I asked.

"It was a combat spork prototype", she said.

"And before that wasn't The Blood War of Tribunus a bit of your doing as well? Something about you running off with his wife and brother for a month to the Island World dimension"?

"It wasn't like that", she said. She wouldn't make eye contact.

"And before that wasn't there the incident that ended up with you being the concubine of the Orcish Kingdoms of Somli", I asked.

"That was a great year", she said. She started blushing furiously.

"So, do you think coming to the Underlands with me would be the best idea", I asked.

"No", she admitted. "But it would probably be fun".

"It may be at that", I mused. Suddenly I stood.

"Truna, would you please assist me", I asked her.

"Well, I really am busy", she said. She was smirking at me. I turned and left without giving her the satisfaction. I would not feed in to her games. At least not when I could have more fun denying her of her victory. Behind me I heard Truna giving orders to Pinky and Sam. As I approached the portal area she had set up I heard her jog up behind me. Without a word I activated the portal and we stepped through.

Arriving back at Center I looked at the time and date display above the portal. It wouldn't be the first time someone had been time slipped traveling to The Depot. Customer service and dedication were no longer mainstays of business.

We made our way along the streets under the strange purple blue sky of Center. The architecture tended to change overnight at times along the whims of a consciousness no one could really understand. But the entire dimension was one intelligence at the hub of the multiverses and probably more; so it did as it wished. We passed races as normal as we, and many more besides. Center was... well the center for every culture that traveled through the multiverse.

We managed to find the entrance to the Underlands between two pubs of questionable service. To be honest we had to duck into the alley rather quickly to avoid a gang of wraiths looking for bodies to steal. Street crime was a different thing in the multiverse. So we may have accidentally found the entrance but still, we were there. Entering the Underlands was easy, getting out may or may not be.

Truna stepped up to a grimy wooden door inset in a brick wall in the alley. She smiled at me and then knocked. Oh no, not that smile. That was the smile she always gave me before she started something. We were about to be in trouble, I just knew it.

"Truna", I started to say as the door opened. A large red skinned pustule demon opened the door. He looked at me then at Truna. His eyes sprang wide.

"Oh, shi", he started but couldn't finish. Truna reached out and smacked the demon so hard it's jaw flew off and bounced down the street. The demon crumpled at the door. Unconscious or dead perhaps, but either way it was definitely out of commision.

"After you", she said and made a great bow while holding the door.

"Oy vey, why", I asked. But I didn't know whether I was asking her, the great cosmos, or my own guardian librarian. I don't think anyone else knew either. She chuckled evilly behind me as I stepped into the Underlands. As one might expect the Underlands resembled a labyrinth of dirty alleys and fetid smells. Slime and grime adorned the streets and walls like mad decorations.

"So", I said and looked around. "Do you have any idea of where to look for the mirror", I asked her. I pulled out a handkerchief to clean my glasses.

"Yep", she said.

"Would you like to tell me where", I asked. Truna loved to edge my patience.

"Oh, I'm sorry", she said grinning. "I was sure I told you".

"Well you didn't", I said.

"Strange", she replied.

"Truna", I almost bellowed.

"Relax, relax", she said. "Don't get your knickers in a twist". But we both knew she wanted my knickers in a twist. It was her greatest amusement.

I sighed and took three deep long breaths. On the fourth I asked, "where are we going"?

"To see your old friend Trogg", she said.

"Trogg", I asked? "Trogg, of all people has the Mirror of Urlrich"?

"You didn't think it would be easy, did you", she asked.

"That's impossible", I said.

"Why", she asked.

"Because if Trogg had the mirror he would be ruling all of Center. His slimy ambition is boundless."

"You're assuming the mirror works for his species", she said. She was being condescending. But she should have been. I had made the fundamental mistake of assuming. Assumptions can be fatal. Look at history. Assumptions have killed a lot of entities throughout the eons. And not a few proprietors.

I turned and led the way down the offal strewn streets. I kept my head up, scanning for threats and those few predators even the threats ran from. The entire place reeked like the end of a bad enema. Just walking down through the area made one feel the need for bathing with a flamethrower to remove the stench.

After maybe fifteen minutes we made it to "Trogg's Bizarre". And it really was bizarre. The interior walls were lined with tent fabric to give customers the illusion that they were in what Trogg thought an old world bizarre should look like. It wasn't clean but it was definitely gaudy. Horrible knick knacks and worse reprints sat stacked along every available surface. The interior conjured fictional ideas of what the yard sale of a clown's grandmother would be like. Maybe that's where Trogg got his merchandise?

"Welcome, my friends, welcome", a cultured voice called out. From within the cornucopia of clutter stepped a large purple skinned goblin like creature. He was wearing a well cut italian suit and round glasses perched on a large aggressive nose. He was a walking dichotomy of appearance.

"How can I help you today", he asked with a feral smile.

"Good evening Trogg", I said. "It is a pleasure to see you again".

"Ah, Mr. Marlow, so wonderful to have a colleague in my delightful shop."

"A colleague, yes of course", I said. I wasn't being snobbish. It's just that there was a large breadth between the items I sold and this... well... this junk. There I said it!

"How can I help you", he asked again.

"We're looking for a silver mirror from one of the adjusted dimensions", Truna said. She had stepped out of one of the side isles and Trogg suddenly looked like he was swallowing his tongue. Could his species have strokes or seizures? I wasn't a Multiverse Medic so I hadn't the foggiest.

"You... You can't be here", he said pointing a finger at Truna.

"I'll go where I please Trogg, or don't you remember", Truna said. I'd swear she was almost purring.

"My apologies good sir", I interrupted. "I can understand your concern but we are only here to procure the mirror. I'm happy to offer a fair price."

"I'll call the Horde if you don't leave", Trogg said. He didn't get a chance to say anything else. Truna reached around me and grabbed Trogg. I stopped to marvel. She had pressed Trogg over her head and was in the process of bending him backwards in what could only be interpreted as a new form of art. Goblin Origami maybe? Trogg was making all sorts of noises as Truna continued to contort him. I couldn't help but find the sight breathtaking and perhaps arousing. She was so beautiful in her casual violence. It was striking. But, there was business to be done.

"Trogg, if you will agree to be civil and discuss business I will ask Truna to put you down", I said.

"Urk" was the elegant response I received.

"Truna, please put Trogg down. He'll remember his manners now", I said.

"Fine", Truna said. She almost looked like she was pouting. She set the goblin back on his feet and even straightened his suit for him.

"Now, may we discuss the mirror", I asked.

"Yes, yes, the Mirror of Urlrich", Trogg said. He was hunched over and started stomping towards a side isle. We followed his grunts and gasps as he walked to a display case somewhere near the center of the melange. He reached into the case and pulled out a silver backed oval mirror with fine filigree carved into every decorative inch of it. It was masterfully crafted.

"Here it is", he said.

"And what's your asking price", I asked.

"Four hundred denarius", he said.

"Sold", I snapped.

"What... but", Trogg stumbled.

"You wouldn't try to haggle your own asking price would you Trogg", I asked. I may have casually patted Truna's bicep as I said it.

"No, I guess not", Trogg said. We exchanged the items. He one mirror and a bill of sale and me four pouches of denarius. Before the situation could go bad Truna and I left the establishment. If anyone heard howls of anguish from the bowels of Trogg's establishment, no one seemed inclined to investigate. Truna kept glancing at me. We walked back through the Underlands and back through half of Center before I gave in.

"Yes", I asked her.

"Why didn't you haggle", Truna asked.

"My dear Truna, why would I haggle over such a fair price", I asked.

"Ok, how much were you offered to find it", she asked. She knew me too well. I wasn't one to miss a sharp trade. She was looking at me suspiciously.

"Alot, my dear Truna, a very great deal", I replied.

"Do I at least get my usual finder's fee", she asked. She was laughing at me. She knew I always paid her double the going fee.

"Of course, as always", I said. We had found our way back to my storefront.

"And thank you for your help. You were amazing as always", I said.

"You're welcome", she said and leaned forward and kissed my cheek. For a brief moment she had hesitated. For a moment it had seemed she was going to kiss me for real.

"Happy Birthday", she called back over her shoulder as she walked away.

I stood in front of my shop and watched her walk away. Wishing she had stayed. Wishing my birthday gift had been more time with her.

"Truna", I called into the darkening night but she didn't hear me. I turned and walked into the shop. I still had to call my client and tell it the good news. Business called.

Curious Statuary

My name is Matthias Mathers Marlow and if you're not yet familiar with me, I am the proprietor of Curious Things. This is my second attempt at recording my adventures which can be found on Central's core computer as well as in many other dimensions. A nice young man named Dave has been teaching me how to work all of this wonderful new technology. I must say it is quite marvelous.

I was contracted by a young demigod of Dave's acquaintance to find a unique piece of statuary. He described it as approximately six inches tall and made of a dark stone similar to obsidian. It was reputed to be a bust of his father. Apparently the statue had been stolen some time ago from a temple dedicated to his father which is now long submerged in the sea. Having had contact with artifacts of the Elder Gods before, I understood the danger of accepting the contract. Money did no one good if they were drooling in the street, after all.

I did some preliminary research and located a historical record of a group of religious zealots who were near the original temple at the time of its sinking. Since the removal of artifacts can sometimes cause a temple to be destroyed, it was not outside the realm to speculate that these zealots may have been the thieves. They had escaped to their new temple located on one of the Beta Earth's in what those of us in the trade call the

Odd Dimensions. These dimensions are places where things are magnified or changed from simple rules of physics to the extreme. On a side note I really do love these computer thingies. It has made my research so much easier. I must remember to visit Sydney at Oracle Dreams and buy Dave a thank you gift!

At any rate, I decided to investigate the site. I left the shop and enjoyed the walk to The Depot. It was a day of sun and clouds, even if the sky was burning purple instead of blue. I entered the Depot and truly wondered at the decor. Large inverted pillars and odd mosaics decorated the walls of the transfer terminal. Odd walkways and queues that went nowhere were a distraction, if not a hazard. The Entities of Entropy really needed to get a better handle on The Depot before some other organization broke in on them. I mean, really!

I found an open portal resonator and swiped my blood token so that I could put in the coordinates. Large warnings flashed around me. The Depot believed in giving you plenty of warning before you did something stupid. Mainly because once you did something stupid, they didn't want to be held liable. Dimensional Civil Liability cases could be a nightmare. I acknowledged the warning and went on through the portal with a dimensional pick up chit for my return. It was expensive but way better than getting there only to find I had no way back.

I exited the portal to find myself standing on a sea shore. Cold rain was pounding down from above and icy breakers crashed into the beach in front of me. The sand of the beach was orange and ran in both directions for as far as I could see. The rain filled sky above me was a sickly gray green.

Large sheer black rocks protruded like jagged teeth from the ocean for miles out to sea. It was a horrific scape to have landed in. I turned around to find a large temple with serrated spires stabbing upward into the sky. The temple was made of the same stone as the jagged rocks of the sea. Every crack and crevice had razor edges meant to draw blood. Strange carvings were etched into most of the exterior, mind bending images that could cause madness if studied too closely.

The entire scene gave off a feeling of dread. I could feel an anxiety running through me, thrumming inside of me. As the wind shrieked past I fancied I could hear a voice. A voice telling me to run into the sea. That drowning in that alien ocean would be better than entering the temple. I shook my sodden self fiercely and started towards the temple. The rain intensified as if it too was trying to warn me away from entering. I reached the first step leading to the doors and heard a scream coming from inside. It was the last terrified scream of a dying man. That last scream to the universe for mercy. I froze and wondered who had just passed and what horrible thing was looking into their eyes as they did.

But I didn't get paid for not completing the job. And I had already invested a good amount of time into this project that I couldn't afford to lose. So, I just needed to muster my courage and stand tall in the face of evil. Bloody hell, I sounded like Churchill. Next I'd be telling myself to keep calm and carry on and charging into the temple shouting "For England" of all things. How bloody trite. Bravery will get you many things, being very dead is at the top of that list.

I walked up the sharp steps to the perfectly etched oval doorway. The door, like everything else on this infernal building, had perfect symmetry. The architecture alone was enough to fray the minds of architects in a hundred dimensions. I reached up to push against the door and could feel a static charge against my hand, burning into me the closer my flesh got to touching the stone. Every hair on my body stood to attention and I had the horrible thought that touching the stone was going to hurt quite a bit. But I did it anyway. Dark sickly visions poured into my mind of a horrible lurking evil entombed within. Horrible thoughts raced through my mind determined to drive me away or send me into the depths of madness. I managed to push through this and in so doing, I somehow pushed the door open as well.

I stood, hyperventilating and in a state of mild shock, in the open doorway attempting to get control of my senses. I was not sure how long I stood there but when I came free of it, the rain had stopped and a fierce wind was blowing harshly through the landscape. My mind felt strange. One time in college a friend had asked me to try a certain mushroom with her, well nevermind, suffice it to say I never did it again no matter how pretty the girl. My mind felt rather like it had after that particular incident.

I forced myself to step through the doorway into the dark interior. A long hall stood before me. The hall was much longer than the temple could possibly have been. Scenes of impossible beings lined every wall, carved into the black stone. The floor looked to be one solid piece of the same stone polished so smooth it reflected the dim light from above. I looked up expecting to see some horrific mural. Instead I found a ceiling of glass. Or rather, not glass but the stone had been shaved so thin as to be translucent. The sickly light of the sky illuminated the dim temple. The effect was beautiful and somewhat creepy, to be honest.

There was a central walkway through the temple. On either side of the walkway were what appeared to be large oval mirrors lined up facing each other, but covered in a gauze or thin fabric of some kind. It looked like a trap, to be perfectly frank.

I started down the walkway and the sounds of my soft footfalls echoed back to me. They seemed magnified somehow. I coughed and listened to the sound come back as a roar. I continued to move, but I could feel deep in my soul that something was watching me. I began to grow increasingly anxious with the feeling. I watched the cloth shrouded mirrors as I passed between each one.

I don't know what caused it. Perhaps a stray breeze from outside, or possibly there was a malignant presence that hated shop owners. But either way death decided to come and watch. From behind me I heard a gentle rustling sound and turned to look. The gauzes were sliding off the mirrors! I wasn't sure what would happen when the effect got to me, but I was willing to take it on faith that the result would be negative. So I ran as hard and as fast as I possibly could. Which is not easy for a middle aged shop keeper, let me assure you. I made the fatal mistake of looking back to see huge clawed arms the size of tree trunks reaching out of the mirrors to grab at me. Which, on the up side, helped me increase my pace significantly. I ran with fear in my soul and terror howling at my heels.

Just as I passed the last set of mirrors I felt a swipe at my back which sent me tumbling. One of the hands had just caught my suit and sent me tumbling. I skidded face first on the smooth stone until my momentum had been spent. I stood quickly looking for threats but seemed to have reached a safe space. I was wrong, but it seemed that way. However, I was growing angry all the same. Not because I was in a terrifying temple, not because I was afraid, not because I had almost died, I was angry because that last clawed hand had ripped my suit. This was my second favorite suit! That was getting added to the expense report, I would be certain.

I had made my way to a central room in the temple. Do not ask me what it may have been called, nothing in this horrible place made sense! The floor sloped downwards on all sides forming a bowl. In the center stood an altar with what could only be the bust my client had asked me to retrieve. Finally, some success on this wretched endeavor.

I stepped into the bowl and felt every muscle in my body go rigid. Screams of terror and torment filled my ears and feelings of utter despair ran through me. I screamed in my mind and fell forward into the bowl. As I collapsed on the stone floor the feelings eased and I was able to breathe again. What had just happened?

I took a moment to lie on the cold stone floor and take mental stock of myself. I didn't feel mad, at least not yet anyway. From the other side of the altar I heard a voice.

"Dude, that looked rough. Are you ok", a masculine voice asked. I looked up to see a long haired man dressed in surf shorts and a bahama style shirt open along bronze skin.

"And who might you be", I asked with my face still against the floor. Politeness is a virtue, no matter the circumstance.

"I'm Dwight", the man said.

"Let me help you up", he said and picked me up taking the time to dust me off.

"What are you doing here", I asked in amazement.

"This is my place, isn't it jammin'", he asked with a huge smile.

"You live here", I asked.

"Only in the summer", he said, like this made total sense. "This place has the best waves this time of year."

"Waves", I asked. Was he speaking English or was I just too fuzzy to tell?

"Totally", he said with a nod. "Why didn't you just knock dude?"

"Knock", I asked. Okay, possibly it was me.

"Yeah, like, I would have totally turned off the alarm system", he said.

"I'm sorry, I didn't know I had set off the alarm", I told him.

"Yeah it's a bitchin' system. Arms that grab people and weird psychic visions, it keeps the townies away", he told me, nodding sagely.

"All of that was just an alarm system", I asked in shock.

"Dude, absolutimundo", he said. "A man's gotta protect his castle."

"Oh dear", I mumbled.

"So what can I do you for", he asked, popping open a canned beverage of some sort.

"I would like to purchase the statue on that altar", I told him and pointed to it. My mind was reeling, it had all been just some sort of alarm?

"Take it", he said.

"What", I asked.

"Take it", he said again. "Thing really weirds me out, you know?"

"Well thank you", I said and handed him one of my cards. "Should you ever need anything please let me know. I'll be sure to return the favor."

"Like totally", he said and gave me another huge smile. I picked up the statue and thanked him again before exiting. Nothing attacked me and the strange echoes were gone. The ancient temple seemed like just another ordinary building now. I walked outside clutching my prize to my chest and activated the recall chit. An alarm system, now really! The things I went through for my clients!

Definitely Not Haunted

Hello again to my loyal clients. I am Matthias Mathers Marlow, the proprietor of Curious Things. I am thoroughly enjoying sharing with you the various experiences of a humble shop's proprietor. Here at Curious Things I aim to please all of my clients thoroughly. To achieve this end I encourage each client to fill out a survey of their experience with my shop so that I can better fulfill their needs.

I would like to offer the results of one such survey to you now to show that while no shop is perfect, we stand by our products. I have already contacted this client and asked for a resolution to his issues, but he states that he is now happy with his purchase. I merely offer this to show that even when a purchase may seem unprofitable on its face, it often works out. And don't forget to stop by Curious Things for all of your unusual needs!

You ever have one of those days that just never goes right? That was today for me. After four alarms I finally managed to roll over enough to realize I was already late for work. Jumping out of bed I threw a cheap kids pastry into the toaster and sprinted for the shower. Five minutes start to finish and no time to shave. I dressed quickly and sprinted for the door. Sprinted back to grab the pastry only to have the filling erupt lava onto my thumb. The filling tried to sizzle straight to the bone. I yelped, threw the pastry and hurried to the door with no time for first aid for my blistered hand. Getting to the door of my cheap little apartment I found a note. A note from my fiance. The note said she just couldn't take it anymore and that she was sorry. She was leaving me.

As I stood stunned with the door partially open my cell phone rang. I was numb and didn't look at the number. "Hello", I said.

"Gavin, this is Linda with HR", a female voice said.

"Hi Linda, I'm on my way now.", I said. I said it knowing it was a total lie. I couldn't think, couldn't feel.

"Gavin, I'm sorry to tell you this but your employment has been terminated", she said.

"But... why", I asked.

"This is your third time being late for work this year and you know corporate policy states you can't have three tardies in a year. I really am sorry", she said.

I hung up the phone. I didn't know what else to do. I didn't have a girlfriend or a job in the space of about five minutes. I just stood there dumbly for who knew how long. I didn't know what to do. I finally took my keys and walked out of the apartment. I didn't know where I was going or which way to go.

I walked for what felt like hours before stopping and leaning against an old building with an ancient wood and glass door. I was coming out of my haze when it started to rain on me. Large fat drops began slamming into me like punches. I looked up to see a sky gone strange. The clouds looked purple and deep blue. What kind of storm was this?

I turned and ran up the three small steps and into the building. Walking inside I found myself in a warm cozy store.

Soft warm brown lights gleamed off hundreds of objects and a number of glass cases. The air had that warm slightly musty smell of antiques and old books.

"Hello, may I help you", a cultured voice asked.

"Sorry, I didn't mean to intrude", I said quickly. "It started raining and I just ran for cover".

"Quite alright young man", the gentleman said and approached me. He was very dapper and well dressed. "I am Matthias Mathers Marlow. Welcome to Curious Things, the shop for the curious and discerning client of all things unusual", he said with a beaming smile.

"Uh, thank you", I said, not really taking it in.

"How may I be of assistance", Mr. Marlow asked.

"Uh, I don't really know to be honest", I said. "Like I said it just started raining and…", I trailed off.

"Ah, I see. And what you do not understand is that no one ever comes in here on their own. They are always seeking something. Even if they do not know it", he said with a small laugh.

Just then a small item in a glass case toppled over. I looked to my left afraid I had just knocked something over. I was always such a clutz. If I had broken anything, how was I going to pay for it?

"Ah, I see", the man stated and walked to the case.

"I'm really sorry, I didn't mean to", I started to say.

"Nonsense, sir. Apparently you were right. You did not know why you were here. Lucky for us, the shop does", the man said absently as he opened the case.

"I'm sorry", I asked questioningly. I had no idea what he was talking about.

"Step over here and see for yourself", he said and pulled an item from the case.

"I'm sorry, but I just lost my job and I really can't afford to buy anything", I told him. But I walked towards him anyway.

"I'm sure we can arrange terms, sir", Mr. Marlow said with a smile. He held a small silver ring out to me. The ring had all kinds of crazy engraving on it. The patterns were so intricate that they seemed to move on their own along the simple silver band.

"That's beautiful", I said in awe. And it was. It looked to be ancient, something from a culture long gone. It was definitely out of my price range, which was zero.

"It would seem, sir, that this ring is what you were inquiring about", Mr. Marlow stated.

"I'm sorry but I really can't", I tried to say.

"Nonsense, young man. I hold here the Ring of Luck worn by ancient kings. Which by the way is definitely not haunted. Yes, not haunted in any way", Mr. Marlow said quickly.

"Not haunted", I questioned. But I wasn't really asking. It was so beautiful. I felt an almost longing to feel it on my finger. A phantom of a memory I could never have had.

"I'm sorry but I can't really afford it", I said.

"Please, allow me to judge the expense", Mr. Marlow said haughtily. "Curious Things is a reputable establishment. We do not fleece our clients".

"I didn't mean to imply", I started but Mr. Marlow was definitely agitated. I guess I had offended him?

"It's all right young man", he said with a sigh. He deflated somewhat. "Allow me to help you. How much do you have on you right now", he asked.

I thought for a minute. "Well, I've got my last hundred dollars in my wallet. But it's all the money I have", I said.

"Tut tut, I'm afraid the cost is one hundred dollars and one cent", Mr. Marlow said. "But what is that on the bottom of your shoe", he asked.

I lifted my foot and, sure enough, there was a penny stuck to the bottom of my shoe. I pried it off in amazement. How had he known that was there?

"So, for the sum of one hundred dollars and one cent I offer you this ring, which is definitely not haunted", he said with an alarming smile. It was the kind of smile that made me want to clutch my wallet and check my bank history.

"Um, okay", I said. I couldn't believe this, what was happening? I handed Mr. Marlow the penny and then dug the one hundred dollar bill from my wallet. Mr. Marlow gently reached out and dropped the ring into my palm.

"Please note that all sales are final and I sincerely hope you enjoy your purchase", he said with another shark smile. He began gently ushering me towards the door. I looked down to find the band on my ring finger. Strange, but I didn't remember putting it on. Before I could even look to see if the rain had stopped I was back outside with Mr. Marlow's, "Thank you for shopping with us", still ringing in my ears.

I looked around and realized I was a block away from my apartment. I turned quickly and found a stone and brick wall of another apartment building stark in the night. How had I gotten here? Where was the door to the shop? What had just happened? I puzzled about this for a minute before giving up and walking back to my apartment. Somehow I felt better than I had in months. The night seemed clearer and had an amazing smell for being this deep into the city. I felt like everything was suddenly right in the universe.

There was a sudden shove between my shoulder blades and I fell forward onto the pavement. The coarse cement scraped my palm as I tried to catch myself. Before I had even landed I felt a sharp blow to my abdomen. Someone had just kicked me in the ribs causing me to roll over onto my back. I couldn't breath and my pulse pounded in my ears.

"Hurry Ricky, get his wallet", a voice said over me.

"What do you think I'm doing", a gruff voice replied.

I felt a sharp tightening from around my finger. My finger where my new ring was. They were trying to steal my ring! Before I could close my hand and protect the ring I heard a voice. A woman's voice.

"Don't worry master, I'll save you", a sexy alto said. I was still having trouble seeing but I could suddenly clearly hear men screaming. I could hear them begging and then a horrible feminine laugh. Loud cracks and muffled whimpers came to my ears but my vision was still blurry. I felt a warm wave of liquid splash over me and the screaming stopped. I managed to sit up only to find the entire sidewalk drenched red.

I cleared my eyes to see the hottest woman I had ever seen standing over me and smiling. Long dark hair and a full on muscle mommy physique that didn't detract from her essential femininity stood before me. I felt like I was going to do the "aoooggaa" staring eyeball thing any second. Damn she was beautiful. I tried hard not to think about why the sidewalk was suddenly red.

"Come my master", she said and lifted me from the ground. I tried to look back to see what had happened but she moved too fast!

"I will clean you up and fix your wounds", she said. I was completely bemused as she carried me up the steps and opened the door to my apartment. She set me down on my feet inside the door.

"Um, I'm sorry, but who are you", I asked.

"I am the spirit of the ring", she said like that should explain everything.

It didn't.

"The what", I asked stupidly.

"The spirit of the ring", she said simply. "Oh, I've waited so long for you", she said and suddenly kissed me.

I just stood there. I'd never had a beautiful woman just grab me and kiss me. Especially with such, ahem, hip action involved. Everything had happened just too quickly. Finally the spirit noticed my discomfort and drew back.

"What's the matter", she asked. "Oh, I'm sorry, do you not like girls?"

"Of, of course I like girls", I stammered. "I just, I mean, I just never."

"It's alright", she said gently and took me by the hand. She started leading me to the bathroom.

"Wait", I said and stopped in the hall. "Who are you and where did you come from", I demanded. Ok, so demanded may have been a little stronger than my actual tone but she did look like she could snap me in half so... Caution may have been advisable.

"I am Nina and I told you, I am the spirit of the ring. And we are betrothed", she said adoringly.

"Wait, the guy said the ring wasn't haunted. And betrothed", I asked. "You mean like marriage betrothed?"

"Why would you ever trust a salesman", she asked like I was riding the spectrum of stupid. "You wear my ring, which means you are my future husband. It's all engraved upon the ring. Did you not read it?" She looked at me like I was the world and my mind was spinning in a vortex of confusion. I latched onto the first idea that came to me.

"You live in the ring", I asked.

"No, silly, I haunt the ring. Actually I'm not living at all." She stopped and pouted. "Do you have a problem with the Living Challenged?"

"The living challenged", I asked. I must sound like an absolute idiot. Was I ever going to catch up on this conversation? Probably not.

"Uh-huh", she said and nodded. "I really prefer that term to some others. Life Disability sounds so negative, Breathing Adverse is misleading, and Lifeforce Impaired just sounds so PC. I just think the Living Challenged represents us better". She turned and headed into the bathroom.

"Are you coming", she asked and motioned me inside.

Mr. Marlow had insisted the ring wasn't haunted. But here was a life size ghost in my bathroom. A very hot, very solid ghost in my bathroom. What was she doing in my bathroom? I heard the shower turn on. Was she going to take a shower? Should I go in? Should I leave? Just how much of a gentleman was I?

"Come on silly", she called. Oh well, let's see how this turned out. Things couldn't get any crazier that was for sure.

"Let's get you a shower and to bed", she said nonchalantly.

"A shower", I squeeked.

"Yes of course, we have to relax you", she said and rolled her eyes.

I gave up. The day had been a wild roller coaster and my brain had finally just run out of the ability to deal. It was closed for business. Stick a fork in me, I was done. I undressed and started to get in the shower. I hissed as the water hit my scrapes. I had forgotten about them until now.

"Oh I am so sorry", she said and yanked open the shower curtain. She grabbed my wrist, totally overlooking the fact that I was naked and pulled my hand to her face. She placed a gentle kiss on the scrape on my hand and it healed almost instantly. I stood in the shower staring at it. It was healed.

"Are there any more", she asked with concern.

"N-n-no", I said. My hand was completely healed.

"Then please finish showering and let's get some rest", she said and smiled winsomely. "You've had a busy day today and tomorrow will be busier."

"It will", I asked.

"Oh yes", she said with a dark tone. "Tomorrow we get revenge."

I woke to the sound of bacon frying. But Christy didn't cook. Wait Christy had dumped me. So who was here?

"Nina", I shouted in sudden realization and sat straight up in bed.

"Are you ok master", Nina yelled as she came running into the room. Her fingernails were claws and she suddenly had fangs and horns protruded from her forehead. She looked around for a threat but it was just me. Naked. I was naked under the sheets. Oh, wow. Uh-Oh. I clutched the sheets tighter around my waist.

"I'm sorry, just a bad dream", I lied. Nina relaxed and her appearance changed back to the woman who had brought me home. Fangs and horns retracted and her claws became simple painted black fingernails again.

"Oh, shoot, the bacon", she said and hurried out.

I quickly got up and threw on a pair of shorts and a T-shirt. No real need to get dressed since I was unemployed. I took a deep breath and walked out into the kitchen. The smells of hot bacon and fresh coffee greeted me. It had been so long since breakfast had consisted of more than a pastry or cheese stick that I stood there in shock for a minute.

"Have a seat master, breakfast will be out shortly", she said with an amazing smile. I stood looking at her for a minute. She was dressed only in tight black gym shorts or tights and a sarong style top. She was so breathtakingly beautiful. I didn't know what she was doing here but I felt that twinge in my stomach. That pull that was way more than lust and usually turned into love. Yea gods, not that. Not so soon after a break up. Like twenty four hours soon. I hadn't even had enough time to be on the rebound yet. But she was just so amazing.

"Can we talk about something", I asked as I sat down.

"Of course", she said and brought me a steaming cup of coffee. I looked at it and it was exactly how I liked it. How had she known?

"Look, um, you can't call me master", I said. "It's just socially unacceptable these days and could cause problems."

"Oh, I didn't realize", she said and looked sad. "What can I call you", she asked hopefully.

"How about Gavin", I said.

"Mmmmmm, Gavin, hhmmmm, what a delicious name for a delicious man. Yes master, I will now call you Gavin", and with that she brought over a steaming plate of eggs and bacon. I shrugged and started eating. It tasted so amazing. Hey, I tried right?

"When you're done you need to get dressed", she said.

"Get dressed", I asked. "Why?"

"I told you silly, we're going to get revenge", and stuck her tongue out at me. Since this wasn't any weirder than anything else in the last twenty four hours I just decided to go with it. Maybe Nina had grudges? She was a ghost so, yeah.

I finished breakfast and went to the shower. Might as well make the best of it. I took my time, showered, shaved, and put on my favorite suit. Maybe if I looked good I'd feel more motivated. Besides, there really wasn't anything to lose was there?

I walked out to find Nina in a black women's business suit. Her hair pulled back in a braid. The look was somewhere between corporate executive and assassin chic. Funny how those two looks are so similar.

"You look very spiffy", she said while eyeing me up and down.

"So do you", I said enjoying the view. "So are you ready for wherever it is we're going?"

"Oh, I am so ready for today", Nina said in a dark voice. It was the kind of voice that could be seductive or threatening depending on the situation.

We walked out of the apartment and were immediately attacked. Not by muggers or wandering mimes. By my neighbors three pound chihuahua. How can so much evil be packed into such a small package? Were they like a never ending node of fury and rage?

The little fiery fuzzball of ferociousness charged at us all tiny teeth and malicious demeanor. Before I could warn Nina she stooped down and speared the fuzzy demon with two of her claws. She then scooped the twitching thing up and brought it to her face. Her jaw unhinged and she shoved the little monster into her mouth, still wiggling. One hard swallow later and it was gone.

"What did you just do", I demanded. I didn't know if I was horrified or amazed.

"I defended us mas- Gavin", she said and burped softly.

"Dexter", a querulous voice called down the hallway. "Dexter, come back here", a woman said. A middle aged woman came out of one of the apartments and towards us.

"Gavin, have you seen Dexter", Mrs. Sanchez asked.

"I think he went that way", I said and she hurried down the hall. I breathed a sigh of relief then saw Nina's face. There was a small bit of blood on the corner of her mouth. I quickly reached out and wiped it away before Mrs. Sanchez returned.

"Did I do something wrong", Nina asked. She looked genuinely puzzled.

"It was just a chihuahua, not a threat", I said to her.

"Those 'chihuahuas' as you call them, are known to harbor some of the greater demons in this dimension. I couldn't take the chance", she said earnestly.

"Ok, fair enough. But no more killing except in extreme circumstances", I said.

"No more killing", she asked. It was clear this was a foreign concept to her. She looked like I had just said something incredibly perverse.

"No more killing except in extreme circumstances", I said firmly.

"I'll try mas-Gavin", she said but she clearly didn't like it. Or maybe she just didn't understand it. I could hear Mrs. Sanchez still calling for Dexter and hurried Nina downstairs.

There was a cab waiting for us. Nina had apparently planned everything already. We both got in and the cab sped off. Neither one of us gave the driver directions so that was creepy by itself. Nina was staring out the window transfixed and I didn't want to interrupt that with a lot of questions. Sometimes waiting was the best solution. I'd know our destination soon enough.

A few moments later we pulled up in front of the office building of my job. Or my former job, rather. Oh man, Nina said we were going for revenge. Did she mean my boss? The HR lady Linda? She just agreed to no killing right? I mean, right? I was a little panicky.

"Um, what are we doing here", I asked.

"I wish to speak to this Linda person and explain that she will change her decision... or else", Nina said and got out of the cab. She handed the driver a hundred dollar bill and he sped away, probably hopeful she wouldn't ask for change. Which was good because I was flat broke anyway. I hustled after her.

"But you just can't barge in and threaten her", I said. Maybe I was pleading a little. I mean, could ghosts go to jail? Could I go to jail if my ghost killed someone? These are life's questions.

"I don't intend to threaten her", Nina said a little nonplussed. We walked into the lobby and rode the elevator to the fifth floor. I was starting to sweat. This could really go all wrong. How had I gotten myself into this? How was I going to get both of us out of it?

We got off the elevator and walked into the foyer of a very posh accounting firm. The receptionist looked up at us and said, "hi, how can I help you", before recognizing me.

Nina walked right up to the receptionist and said, "Hi, we're here to see Linda with HR, please". The receptionist went from slightly ruffled to completely agreeable in like three seconds. I couldn't see Nina's face but she couldn't be in scary mode if the receptionist was being that calm. Maybe scary and sexy weren't her only two modes?

"Of course", the receptionist said and smiled at Nina. It wasn't a come hither look but it was close. That answered that question. Having already had a fantasy or two about Nina myself I really couldn't blame the receptionist.

As the receptionist picked up the phone to call HR, Nina turned to me and smiled. Definitely couldn't blame the receptionist. Nina's smile lit up her entire face and her eyes glittered like jewels. A lesser person would have fallen to their knees and groveled. But not me, nope. I was made of sterner stuff. And no, the counter holding me up had nothing to do with it. Nothing at all. The receptionist sat the phone down and looked at us.

"Security will be down momentarily to take you to HR. And if I can help in any way, please let me know", she said. There was a lot of emphasis on the phrase help in any way but again I couldn't blame her. And when did we get security?

The elevator dinged and a walking mountain stepped out. I didn't know how he fit on the elevator in the first place. He probably had to duck to fit. The guy's chest was so broad it probably had its own zip code. Where did they find this guy, behemoths are us? Was there a Kaiju factory I didn't know about?

"This way", the walking gargantuan said. Oh my god, we were going to die. I was going to crack. His voice squeaked! Giant body and such a high pitched voice. I don't know why it struck me so hilariously but it did. He was going to crush me with one thumb and I was going to die laughing. Literally! I held it in as Nina walked on my foot. My laughter turned to a yelp of pain and I was grateful. We joined the colossus in the elevator and it was a very... intimate... ride due to the lack of space. Two floors up and the doors opened again. I won't say we were ejected but the lack of available room probably made it seem that way. Gigantor followed us out and directed us to Linda's office.

We knocked and the giant stayed in the lobby as a soft voice called, "come in".

Nina walked in first and stopped dead. If I hadn't paid attention I would have plowed into her. Linda from HR stood behind her desk and Mr. Huxley, the owner of the firm, stood silhouetted against the large bay window overlooking the front of the building. He turned and smiled. His eyes centered on Nina.

"It's good to see you again", he said to her. He was a strong athletic man, clean shaven with dark hair and a hint of silver at his brows. His suit probably cost more than my car and his smile gleamed in the light.

Linda threw a handful of dust at Nina and she screamed and fell to the floor. It looked like dust but it was causing Nina terrible pain. She writhed and howled as her fingers turned back to claws and dark horns erupted from her head. Her hair covered her face but I could see one eye glowing violet with rage as she glared at Mr. Huxley.

"What did you do", I yelled at Linda.

"You should be grateful Gavin", Huxley said. "She is freeing you from a terrible plight."

"And what plight is that", I demanded.

"Why, being the bearer of that ring, of course", Huxley said. "Now, hand it over", he said and moved towards me.

Ok, I had to think. Did I have to worry about the human mountain? No, they would have told him not to interrupt. I'd never been in a fight in my life. Think, think, think! There was a crystal pitcher of water and some glasses on a credenza behind me. I didn't know if this would work but what else could I do?

I snatched the pitcher from the credenza and threw the water onto Nina. The water sizzled and Nina howled. She howled with a thousand voices and Huxley screamed at me. I turned just in time to see Linda try to stab me with a large dagger. I don't know what made me do it. I didn't mean to do it. I smashed Linda in the face with the water pitcher.

Linda went down. And I mean she went down hard. But what I wasn't expecting was for her to land on her knife. She shrieked once, stiffened, and then went limp except for small jerks of her hands and feet. She was... she was dead. I had killed her.

Huxley and Nina both looked at Linda's body and then Huxley reached for his briefcase. Before he could get to it Nina was on him. I don't know if it was the water flushing the dust away or Linda suddenly dying but Nina was free and ready for violence.

"You killed me, you locked me in that ring", Nina said and hoisted Huxley into the air with one hand around his throat.

"Nina", Huxley gasped then began choking.

"It's only fair I kill you isn't it", and with that she squeezed. Huxley's head came off in a small eruption of blood and gore. Nothing like what you see in the movies. Nothing at all. Huxley's body tumbled to the floor and his head landed and bounced with a soft sound. I thought I was going to puke. I looked at Nina as she stood, gory and gorgeous, silhouetted in the light.

"Never date a wizard", she said and turned to me. Her face became loving.

"Come my master, let us be free", she said as she scooped me off the floor.

"Definitely not haunted my butt", I mumbled as we left the office and started towards a whole new life. What would that be like?

Slithering Matchmaker: First Day

By: Scarlett Grim

Covered in guts, ooze, and a whitish mucus like substance that came out of some undetermined hole on some undetermined thing I winced knowing the smell of this was never coming out of my hair. The name is Kari, and you better not be wondering how I ended up sitting in the back corner of this godless bar watching these freaky creatures getting even freakier. But, just in case you are, here is how it started.

Once I was a field journalist for a newspaper and app news outlet called IDiety. The place for all the supernatural happenings and incidents. I was one of the only humans allowed to work there as part of the Human Inclusion Program. The goal was to get supernatural beings used to humans because humans really are the most terrifying monsters in the mutliverse.

To make a long story short I made it six years, six months and five freaking days before I was canned. All because I reported the truth about a car accident between a werewolf and a shrunken head man. I reported the truth, which was that the werewolf had changed in the middle of the road and the shrunken head man couldn't get out of the way in time.

With all the werewolf rights activists breathing down our throats, IDiety wanted me to spin it to where there was some cause other than the obvious. I just couldn't do that. My readers depended on me for my journalistic integrity. As a human if I got caught lying it could literally be the death of me. They promised to keep me safe, but if I learned one thing as a human child, trust no one and watch your own back.

Needless to say my story accidentally aired with the truth because the editor thought I had been sufficiently frightened, and they fired me. Instantly my replacement went on the air. Kandi with a K, was an auburn haired green eyed pale bombshell. According to the readers her thick thighs were perfect for any man that had asphyxiation kinks. It didn't hurt that the girl's jugs were the size of some pretty decent cantaloupes and her voice sounded like honey on the microphone. Fucking succubi, you cant compete with them and you cant join em.

So after my humiliating departure, I struggled for months on Nightdeed. Being a human in this job market really is a bitch. Plus after you work here you can't go back to doing a normal human job because you wouldn't have any of your memories or job experience. Which meant hours of staking down job leads on the number one search engine for the nightbound and the hidden entities of the muliversal realms. Most jobs don't hire humans unless they sign contracts bartering their souls. Employers felt that there wasn't much more to offer other than that, I'm afraid.

Just as I was about to give up, I received an email from this place called *Slithering Matchmakers*. Turns out they needed a writer for their date reviews. Seemed easy enough and humans were encouraged to apply. I tried it, but figured I wouldn't get it as "some receptionist duties may be required". About a week after I applied though, thats when the email was just sitting there.

Good morning Kari,

We are hopeful that you are still looking for employment and would love to have you come in for your first day at the office. 666 Damnation Dr. Suite A., around 8:00 am Center Time. The response from your previous supervisor was amazing and they already sent us sample columns.

No need to worry about the reason for your termination, we value honesty here at Slithering Matchmakers, in fact our brand is built on it. So if you're interested please respond that you will be attending tomorrow. Please do not worry about compensation or benefits as they will be discussed with you upon your arrival before you begin work. Let us know if you have any questions.

Love is our business,

Maddi.

I was ecstatic, no shitty interview, the IDeity review of them was pretty high, and I could write again. No magical toilet cleaning for Kari. No dresscode from the looks of it and all the pictures showed a pretty humanoid staff. If I was lucky this was my dream job.

On my first day I arrived early and met one of the owners, Maddi. She was so sweet, and so stylish. Maddi was a decently tall female creature, with beautiful olive skin. She wore these deep tinted glasses that really shaded her eyes, but you didn't notice because she had this dreamy voice. The only thing that threw me off was the wiggling headwrap. It made no sense, but I didn't ask.

The pay was fantastic. Twice what I made at IDeity, and I got a clothing budget with cleaning expenses paid weekly. A company card to buy myself lunch or dinner at whatever establishment I was writing at, and a company car to get from one place to another because I didn't have one. She even gave me a company phone and the front desk was mine to decorate however I wanted within the monthly budget she planned to give me. The benefits were pretty standard; dental, unhealth,and afterlife insurance, all covered by Slithering Matchmaker of course.

Like a dumb ass, I didn't ask for specifics, I just accepted the job. With all the paperwork complete Maddie began the tour of the shop. She told me she would show me around then we would talk about what and how I would write. The excitement filled me as we made our way to the first door. It was a beautiful oak door with a copper plate on it that read "Complaints".

The room was stunning. Filled from floor to roof with beautiful plants from all over the world. The stone path led to a thick white tree that had been laid on its side to fashion a desk. Very organized and clean was my first impression of this department, but fear struck me as a deep husky voice spoke from a distance.

"Slithering Matchmakers Complaints Department, how can we amaze you today?" The voice came from a very hairy, very large minotaur. The name badge read Steve, but who was paying attention. He was wearing pants and a blazer. I had freaking seen everything, a minotaur in pants. Maddie got Steve's attention with a small wave.

"It's just me and the new receptionist Kari. No need to sound so polite, but I would like you to warn Eurina that we are here so that she doesn't pop in for a visit unannounced." Matti smiled at him and I could swear I saw Steve blush. She had this calming but stern way about her, and I was honestly a little jealous.

Maddie walked me around the beautiful and lush garden and the smell was orgasmic. We made our way to a beautiful water feature in the middle of the room that I was pretty sure was real jade. The room was so elaborate, I honestly couldnt believe we were still indoors and the statues in the area were so lifelike. Although I didnt understand at the time why they had such pinched and ugly expressions.

Around the corner came Eurina, a sweet looking mousey individual, she had some of the same striking features as Maddie but without glasses and quite a bit shorter. Less stylish too. I didn't see how anyone could complain to her. She was just too cute to look at.

"It's rude you know to judge me on my height. I might look small and innocent, but I am darkness," she hissed at me. Confusion painted my face as I was sure I hadn't said that out loud.

"Eurina makes all these lovely statues, and handles the complaints with her sorting assistant Steve. She only handles the hardest cases and we like that she can read minds. It helps solve the issues so much faster that way." Maddi smiled and hugged Eurina tightly.

"She doesn't bite I promise. She's just cranky" the obvious sisterly connection was there and it was nice to see such a happy work environment. Eurina explained to me how the department worked. Steve handled the sorting, some people just tried again and others needed someone to yell at.

The tougher cases went to Eurina with a weekly report being sent to Maddi. It looked like a nice relaxing job. I hadn't forgotten that she had just wigged out on me. I was choosing not to remember.

The same thing happened with the dragon in billing, the sphinx in records, and the hydra in the phone room. The phone room creeps me out to this day. I don't go in there. Calls that go on in there are horrific even by my standard and make an X rated porno look like a kids movie. Moving on.

The woman in collections was just as beautiful as Maddi. Serah was confident and poised. Her room looked much less extravagant than some others, and just had black walls with a red door. Side note, I have never made it in there, but once I did hear a man screaming and begging for his life to the sounds of chains and laughter. Had to be a movie though because I'm pretty sure Serah was the one doing all the laughing.

Finally we made it to my desk where, after all I had seen and heard, the boring part began. This was when I found out that I would be accompanying the clients on their first dates to ensure the matches were a success. I would also be responsible for helping them fill out their new client paperwork. My car was also to be used on occasion to transport clients too nervous to drive to their first dates.

Little did I know that the next week would begin my life of endless bad hair days, discoveries of nightmares, and I'm pretty sure I'm in love with a vampire. Enthralled is also a possibility but that doesn't matter. I'm in too deep to get out now, and I should have run after my first matchmaking session with Cthulhu's illegitimate love child and a Cherub named Alex.

Find More Books In The Hellhound-verse

Visit Hellhoundsrun.com

<u>The Nivaari Series</u>
Nihil - Paranormal Thriller
<u>Exploits Series</u>
Exploits of an Underpaid Supernatural Bartender - Paranormal Humor
<u>Second Sypher Wars</u>
Gaeth's Redemption -Fantasy Adventure
<u>Finding Love Series</u>
From Hell and Back: A Journey From Loss to Love Again- spicy and melancholy poetry

Did you love *Exploits of an Underpaid Supernatural Bartender*? Then you should read *Gaeth's Redemption*[1] by Charles M. Brown!

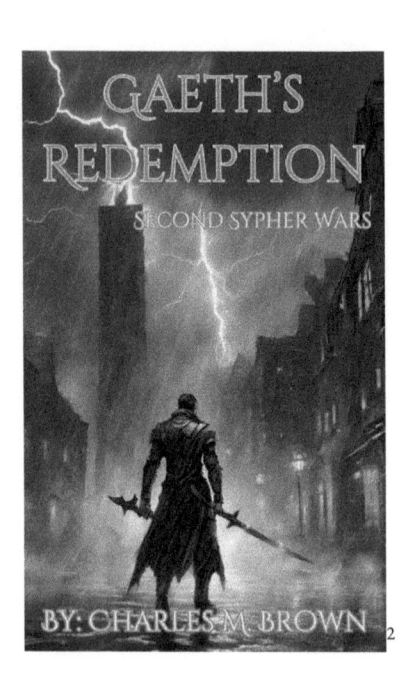

"You always warned me that being queen would mean my death." - Simone

A romantic war story that starts when Gaeth a man with a war-torn heart, meets Simone a woman too afraid to become queen. With losses accrued on both sides, the couple struggles to find a balance between the magical chemistry within them and the catastrophic destiny that awaits them. Gathe's Redemption features yokai, witches, descriptive battles, and

---

1. https://books2read.com/u/4EB7Gg

2. https://books2read.com/u/4EB7Gg

some spicey scenes all coming together to show that the lines of war and lust are not all that different.

Read more at https://www.hellhoundsrun.com/.

About the Author

Charles M. Brown is the creator of the Hellhoundverse, a universe where the impossible becomes possible, and the adventures are endless. The Hellhoundverse uses a mixture of media containing adventures through creepypastas and novels alike. These adventures explore all walks of life within the universe while meeting the entities within. Charlie also enjoys writing poetry that explores deep human emotions within everyday occurences. From leaving abusive relationships to finding real love, enjoying the simplicity of a front porch and good blues. He spent over twenty-five years in public service as a Law Enforcement Officer and 911 Telecommunicator before rediscovering his dream of writing. He has previously won several awards for his poetry in his youth and is greatly enjoying bringing his new works to life. Follow my socail media links at : linktr,ee/hellhoundsrun

Read more at https://www.hellhoundsrun.com/.